WILLOW'S JOURNEY
DAUGHTERS OF SAMUEL FOX, BOOK FIVE

CHAR CAULEY

BLUSHING BOOKS

Published by Blushing Books
An Imprint of
ABCD Graphics and Design, Inc.
A Virginia Corporation
977 Seminole Trail #233
Charlottesville, VA 22901

©2018 by ABCD Graphics and Design, Inc. and Char Cauley

All rights reserved.

No part of the book may be reproduced or transmitted in any form or by any means, electronic or mechanical, including photocopying, recording, or by any information storage and retrieval system, without permission in writing from the publisher. The trademark Blushing Books is pending in the US Patent and Trademark Office.

Char Cauley
Willow's Journey

EBook ISBN: 978-1-61258-924-4
Print ISBN: 978-1-61258-988-6

Cover Art by ABCD Graphics & Design

This book contains fantasy themes appropriate for mature readers only. Nothing in this book should be interpreted as Blushing Books' or the author's advocating any non-consensual sexual activity.

WILLOW

Willow stood in the corner of her bedroom. Her hands in front of her, her fingers twisted in agitation. Her long, wheat-colored hair was in a braid hanging down to her hips, and her bright violet eyes shone with unshed tears. Her head was bowed in abject misery. How was it she was here again, and this time, there was no getting out of a spanking?

The last time, she had looked so pathetic that even her papa felt bad for her and let her go with a warning. The warning stated that the very next time she did not wait for him to go with her to the traveling sales wagon, the next time she bought anything from any of the many traveling sales wagons, without him, she was in for a hard spanking. Willow stomped her bare foot. Darn it; she had wanted those cast iron pans and they were so cheap. The man said he only had three left, so she couldn't wait for Lou. As soon as she had put the fire under them to make his breakfast, they had cracked. Having been made with inferior cast iron, they were worthless. That is where her papa was now, getting her money back. He had told her to undress and stand in the corner until he returned. A tear slipped down her cheek as she waited for him to come home again. Suddenly, she heard the door shut and footsteps leading to their bedroom.

Lou stood in the bedroom doorway looking at his little Willow. He threw the dollar bill on the bed and walked over to her. Putting his hand on her slender shoulders, he turned her and, with a finger under her chin, lifted her face to look into her eyes. Her tears always tore into his heart. He had promised her a spanking, and a spanking she was going to get. He pulled her to the bed and sat her on his lap as he picked up the dollar.

"Another dollar into your piggy bank for the orphanage. Do you know that man was a criminal? Gabriel and I hauled him to the jail, and when we collect the reward, I will put our usual ninety percent in your savings and give you the ten percent for the orphanage. How many times have I told you that many of these men are using their wagons to outwit the law? They make enough money to keep moving. Do you know that he said he learned about the little nurse from one of the other wagons he had met on his way to town? All of the traveling salesmen know what a sucker you are. Do you know he could have snatched you as well as your money? A lot of these men are dangerous and yet you insist on buying their junk, instead of going to the mercantile."

Willow looked at her angry husband. "But, Lou, most of the time, they have much better prices."

"Because it is junk, Willow!" he shouted. He stopped to breathe, closing his eyes to control his anger. With a deep sigh, he got control of himself again, "Willow, we have more money than we will ever spend. You do not need to seek bargains. I will not have you putting yourself in danger for a few pennies. You are too precious to me. I have enemies who would pay some unscrupulous person good money to snatch you for ransom or to hurt you, to get back at me. I know I have talked to you about this. Am I not communicating this in the king's English, so you understand?"

Willow felt the tears fall and saw them drop on her husband's fingers. "I am sorry, Lou. I promise never to do this again,"

Lou shook his head. "No, Willow, not this time, I allowed you to get away without a spanking last time, and look what happened. You repeated your mistake, not a month later. You leave me no choice but to spank you hard." He looked into her eyes to make sure she understood why he was going to spank her.

More tears slipped from her eyes. "But, Lou, I don't want a spanking," she finally wailed into his shirt.

Lou gave her a hug before he continued. "Willow, do you trust me not to really hurt you? Not to leave any marks or to ever hit you anywhere but on your bottom or your thighs? Look at how much bigger than you I am. Do you think you could stop me from really hurting you if I chose to? I would never cause you serious harm. I love you more than my own life. That is why I need to make sure this spanking puts a mark on your mind to never do this again."

Willow nodded her head in defeat. "I trust you, Papa." She got up and put herself over his knees, laying the top of her body on the bed with her legs hanging down.

Lou put her where he wanted her, with her bottom in the center where he could get at it better. He gently rubbed her soft cheeks. It never failed to amaze him how smooth her skin was, how white it was and how apple red it would become. He reached over and gave Willow her stuffed bear, Winkey. So named because one of the eyes was missing. One of the orphans had given it to her. She quickly hugged it to her.

"Hang on to Winkey and don't let go, or I will have to hold your hands. I am going to give you twenty spanks. Ten for lying to me when you said you would not go to the tinker man again and ten for disobeying me."

Willow held tightly to Winkey and replied, "Yes, sir, but please, Papa, don't spank me too hard."

Lou chuckled. "Little one, you know you have no say in this. I have to make sure you never do this again."

With that, he began, starting out easy and not too hard but increasing the intensity and the speed. The sting and burn turned to heat. It flowed down to her woman parts, which confused Willow, but she accepted it. The heat began to build until she began to wiggle her bottom and try to get away from it, her arm loosening around Winkey. But a word of "No" from Lou and she again hugged her stuffy tightly again. Her face was in the blanket as she began to softly sob. He was relentless continuing up and down her bottom, left, right and then down. The heat burst into a flame sometime between ten and fifteen. The fire on her bottom danced with his hand. She was sobbing hard now and kicking her feet.

Lou stopped at sixteen. "Only four more, Willow. On your sit spots, and they will be harder to bear. Then we are finished.

She was sobbing too hard to talk so she nodded, and he finished with four of the hardest spanks, all on her sit spots, to remind her every time she sat down that she was not to go alone to the traveling sales wagon, or the tinker man as they were sometimes called.

He gently lifted her to sit on his lap, careful to put her red-hot bottom between his legs and not on his scratchy jeans. He put her head on his massive chest and rocked her, crooning soft words of love and forgiveness. He watched with a smile as her little thumb crept towards her mouth, her bear in one arm. Just as it reached her mouth, he gently pulled it down and waited. A split second later, the "Na!" he was waiting for came, and the thumb went back into her mouth.

She was an exceptional nurse, professional, intelligent and caring. Lou felt so lucky he had found someone who needed him to be her papa—to take the load off her small shoulders sometimes, and to keep the many people who would take advantage of a woman like her away. She had no defenses against people who would use her. She was raised in an orphanage and had no comprehension of how people really were. Many were good, hard working people, but he also knew some who just liked to take advantage of the weaker.

Sometimes, like when she lost a child in the clinic not long ago, she just needed a papa. He had found her that day when he came home, curled on the bed, crying her heart out. He picked her up and rocked her in the rocker and just held her until she fell asleep. Only then, did he put her to bed.

Lou had the urge to be a papa from an early age but never found the right woman. He had waited for his little Willow. He had a dream one night when he was younger of a little girl just like her. He knew he would find her because his dreams usually came true. Maybe it was his photographic mind playing tricks on him. He wasn't sure why, but they did.

Yep, he was a lucky man, and he knew it. He also knew he and Gabe had many enemies who would think nothing of hurting or killing anything they loved for revenge. They had put many men away in their lives. The prisons were full of dangerous men Lou and Gabe had sent there.

Lou was six-foot-five, with brown hair and whiskey-colored brown eyes. Many men feared him and with good reason. Some had seen their own death in them. The same with Gabe. His cold blue eyes could strike terror in any man. He was a master of disguises and human behavior. He knew what little tells meant. He could tell with great accuracy if someone was lying, just by actions.

They learned at the knee of Hawk and Samuel to be the best Pinkerton men the government had. They commanded a great respect amongst judges and law enforcement.

Lou started lunch while Willow slept, just sandwiches and milk. He went to wake his wife. Sitting on the side of the bed, he brushed the stray hair from her cheek before he gave her a gentle kiss.

She turned to her back to look up at her husband before she remembered her sore bottom. With a moan, she turned off to her side. Her hand went up to him to pull him down for kiss, but he stood.

"You know the rules, little girl. No pleasure after a spanking." He chuckled at her as she began to pout.

"I made you a sandwich. I have to go to the sheriff's office for a conference with Gabe. Something is going on that we need to know about. Samuel and Hawk will be there, also. I will be done before supper, so why don't I meet you at Kayla's, tonight? We can dine with Gabe and Missy."

"But Lou, I need you now."

Lou patted her bottom before leaving her without answering her.

As soon as he left and she heard him locking the door, her hand went under the blankets. If he wouldn't take care of her needs, she would do it herself. It wasn't as good, but what Lou didn't know wouldn't hurt him. Her hand went to her sopping pussy, gathering her juices. She found her love button, as Lou called it, and began rubbing up and down, her fingers slippery from her own juices. Harder and faster until she felt the tightening inside—her muscles tightening in anticipation. Her head was back on the pillow, her mouth open, emitting moans. Finally, the explosion she expected, the stars she reached for. She lay on the pillow, a smile of complete satisfaction on her face. She laid in bed a second more to catch her breath and to give her heart time to slow back to normal. She got up and walked to the water bowl to clean herself before she again dressed. Then she walked to the kitchen with a huge smile on her face. Yes, her bottom still hurt some, but all was right in her world. She ate her sandwich standing up. When she was finished, she decided to make Lou his all-time favorite apple pie for dessert. She had plans for her husband, tonight. She daydreamed of all the things he could do to her. Lou never allowed pleasure after a spanking, but that night was always amazing. He more than made up for it.

THE ROSES

Lou walked to Kayla's to meet his wife with bad news. The men wanted to wait for the others before telling it, so it needed to be told only once. Samuel was bringing Suzy, and Hawk was bringing Little Bird, and he had already stopped by Jarod's to invite Autumn and him. Since Summer was there, he invited Summer and Mark as well. Gabe was rounding up Storm, since he was not only family but also now the district attorney. His wife, Wynter, was big with child and was at home, but he knew that Storm would relay the message. He gave Willow a kiss and explained to her that they were waiting for the others before they ordered.

As the others filtered in, Willow became nervous. They never had one of these family meetings unless there was trouble. It always meant the girls were under house arrest or needed to go partnered. It restricted them. She had a career she had worked hard for. Missy also had a career, and being under restriction made it harder for them to do their jobs. Willow was an orphan; she had overcome so much in order to get where she was in her career, she didn't want anything to stand in the way of it.

Finally, when Storm had arrived and everyone was seated, the waitress came to take their orders. Kayla sat in an empty chair to listen, so she could take the news back to Tom.

The food was delicious, as usual, but everyone was so on edge, it was hard to have much of an appetite.

Finally, after the waitress cleared the table and brought the coffee, Samuel began. "We have had a telegram from the governor. Willard and Terry Rose have escaped from the Yuma State Prison. These men are the most dangerous I have ever known. They are brothers and sociopaths. They feel no guilt or remorse for killing, and they like to torture their victims. The more they see you scream in pain, the more they enjoy it."

Lou jumped in as everyone listened carefully, "Gabe and I captured them, finally, and had them sent to prison. They have been ranting and raving, apparently, about paying us back."

Gabe looked at all the women, his gaze landing on every single one of them before he spoke. "They tortured a woman and killed her baby, just because she refused their advances."

The women gasped in shock at that news, and that is when Hawk spoke up, " We insist you women go in pairs wherever you go. You know the routine; we have had to use it before."

Willow spoke right up before Missy could begin, "We have careers. Missy teaches school, and I am a nurse. Now, while I can go to work with Jarod, Missy cannot."

Samuel cleared his throat, so he could be heard loud and clear, "You girls will be coming to stay with me and Suzy for a while." When he saw the both of them begin to get out of their chairs to leave, he also stood, along with Lou and Gabe. "You *will* be staying with me!" He left neither of them any doubt that it would happen.

Lou took Willow's arm and then looked at Missy. "Gabe and I are going out to meet them and, hopefully, catch up to them before they get to Wyoming. As far as we know, they don't know we are married. We are going to stop them before they find out we are. We will be gone for maybe a month or more, maybe less. It depends on if luck is on our side, but we need to stop them before they get to Buffalo."

Gabe took Missy's arm also and added, "The longer these men are loose, the more people will die." He lifted Missy's face to look him in the eye. "They killed a young mother. Not fast or easy, either. It took her a while to die. In front of her baby."

Missy's eyes filled with terror. "But these men are really dangerous. Gabe, what if something happens to you?"

Willow looked up into Lou's eyes. She saw doubt for the first time. "You are not sure you can catch them again. I see it in your eyes. What if they catch you and torture you?" Tears filled her beautiful eyes.

Lou pulled her into his arms before he sat back down and pulled her onto his lap. "Darlin', Gabe and I are the best. Didn't Samuel and Hawk teach us all they knew? Don't worry about us. We will catch them, not just for our family, but because these men are too dangerous to be let out in society."

"How hard was it to catch them the first time, Lou?"

Lou looked down at the floor, unwilling to look Willow in the eye for the first time in their marriage.

Gabe spoke up then. "One of them almost killed Lou. He shot him and left him for dead. I can't lie to you two. We had a hell of a time. Just because they are sick individuals doesn't mean they are not cunning as hell. These men are sneaky and smart, and they don't care who gets hurt or killed. I was lucky I found Lou and got him to the doctor in time. Very lucky."

Tears fell on Willow's cheek as the family watched helplessly. "I don't want you to go, Lou," she wailed.

Lou hugged her tightly. "That is not an option, little one. These men cannot stay on the loose. Not just for our sake but for anyone that they come in contact with. I promise to be careful. I have a reason to live and come home now."

Samuel spoke up, "They do not need to be burdened with the extra worry of your safety. You will come home with us. School hasn't started, and I have already talked to Jarod. Jennifer will work extra hours for a while and, hopefully, it won't be for long."

Both girls reluctantly agreed, and the other men promised to make sure their wives had escorts whenever they went out.

"The sheriff has a deputy to help with seeing to the wives, if we need an extra escort for something," Hawk told them.

∽

AFTER THEY RETURNED home and Lou made sure the doors were locked, he turned to Willow.

"I have a powerful need of you, wife. Gabe and I will leave at first light. Samuel and Suzy will come for you before we leave. Please, Willow, behave for them. They are only trying to protect you. It eases my mind to know you are safe."

He lifted her in his big, strong arms and carried her to the bed, where he put her on her feet and began to undress her.

"Just like opening a present at Christmas."

Willow giggled, trying to forget for just a few hours that her husband was putting himself in terrible danger.

"Why is it when I put myself in danger I get a spanking and, when you do it, that is just the way it is?"

Lou chuckled. "That is because, little one, I am the papa and you are the little one who needs protecting."

He slowly unbuttoned her dress and watched as it pooled at her feet. He let the straps of her slip fall down her arms as his hands lingered near her breasts. He then helped her step over her clothes before he lifted her face first onto the bed. Helping her onto her elbows and knees with her bottom facing him, he pulled her hips to the edge of the bed before he stepped out of his own clothes. He put his cock next to her opening before quickly impaling himself. With a moan, she pushed back. She spread her legs, so he could go even further. He held her hips to steady her as he pounded into her— faster, further, harder, with a desperation, until he could feel her near her limit. With a howl from both of them, they both came apart at the same time. Lou continued to pump every last drop of himself into his wife, hoping, this time, they made a baby. In case something went wrong, she would have something of him to keep her company on the long, lonely days. He hoped it didn't happen that way, but he was a realistic man. He had seen too much death not to be. He gently laid her on the bed, making note of the condition of her bottom before he turned her to her back. Just slightly pink. He smiled at the sight. He had done a good job, and he was sure she would remember to stay away from the traveling sales wagon. He walked over to the washstand and gathered the washcloth, then he cleaned both her and himself before he put more wood on the fire. It was starting to get chilly at night already. Lou took Willow twice more during the night.

The next morning, before dawn, Samuel and Hawk and their wives came to take Missy and Willow home with them. Lou and Gabe hated to let them go, but they knew the sooner they took care of this, the sooner they could come home. With a long kiss, Lou let Willow go with Samuel.

Gabe and Lou mounted up after packing their saddlebags and rode out for the train station in Rawlins. They would ride the rails until they got to the Utah state line. That is where the sheriff thought Willard and Terry would be. It would be a starting point. Every lawman in the area was on the lookout and had orders from the governor to relay the message to him if they were spotted. The boys would check at the sheriffs' offices for updates.

SAMUEL'S RULES

The girls were under strict instructions not to leave the ranch, for any reason, under penalty of Samuel. They were not to even leave the area around the house.

Willow was helping Suzy with meals and laundry, but it was soon apparent that Suzy had her own way of doing things and Willow was more underfoot than helping. Willow decided to do some exploring. The first couple of days, she just stayed close to the ranch house, wandering through the woods, close enough to hear Suzy calling for her if she was needed. Every day, she wandered a little further until she came to a small stream. She could see fish swimming and the water looked so cool, she couldn't resist taking her shoes off and dangling her feet in the water. She leaned back with her eyes closed until she felt someone behind her. She opened her eyes to see Brenden standing behind her with two fishing poles.

"I knew you would find my favorite fishing hole if you kept wandering long enough." He handed her a baited pole and they sat and fished most of the afternoon. Brenden talked about when he was a kid growing up on the ranch and having Samuel and Suzy for parents.

Willow talked about how frightened she was for Lou and Gabe.

They caught supper that night and agreed to come back and fish again the next week. It helped to have someone with sympathy to talk to.

Suzy made a fuss of all the fish they would have for supper and how grateful she was for it. Missy brought in some vegetables from the garden she had been working in all day. The kitchen was full of praise, and everyone had a great meal that night.

Brenden promised to come the next day and show them Wynter's pond, so they could do a little swimming. The days were still very warm, and the cool water sounded so good. The girls were so excited, they had a hard time settling down that night, until they heard Samuel scolding from the kitchen. The next afternoon, right after lunch, Brenden showed up with two horses and off they went to spend the afternoon doing absolutely nothing but having fun.

Suzy knew Brenden was trying to keep the girls' minds off the danger their men were in. It seemed to be working. She also knew Brenden had work to do but was making time for something more important to him.

The girls returned with rosy cheeks and laughter that could be heard from the stable. Brenden stayed for supper before he returned home to his wife and the work of his ranch.

By the end of the first week, the girls had pretty much explored most of the ranch that was close enough to explore.

Suzy took them to the graveyard when she went and explained that Spring and Autumn's parents were there, along with her parents and one baby who was stillborn. Suzy explained she had been pregnant several times, but one time, just before Shaun was born, she had carried a child into the seventh month. She explained to them how it had almost killed her. The baby was perfectly formed but so tiny that it could not live on its own yet. Willow put her arms around Suzy as the tears fell while she told the story.

"Samuel made me take some awful tasting medicine after that. He didn't want me to try to have any more children. He didn't want to lose me, you see. I disobeyed him and threw it away and didn't tell him. When he went to get it, it was too late. We had made a baby, and that was Shaun." She stood from the ground and brushed off her skirts after she placed flowers on all the graves, and the girls wandered back to the house.

Willow had to know. "How did you dare to defy Samuel? I would be terrified."

Suzy smiled. "I wanted a baby so badly. I had Spring and Autumn and, later, Summer, but I wanted my own. I wanted to give this one gift of love to Samuel. The gift only I could give him. I knew in my heart, this was going to be the one I could keep."

Willow and Missy nodded their heads. "I feel the same way," they both said at once.

Once they returned home, the girls all helped with supper, and just as Samuel walked in the door, they had the meal on the table.

Samuel stood in the doorway with a tired smile on his face. "That smells wonderful. I am a lucky man."

Suzy smiled happily as she walked over to Samuel and raised her face for a kiss. "I made your favorite pie."

"You are a good wife, darlin'. I am *really* a lucky man."

Both girls giggled as the couple stood in the doorway and kissed.

Samuel gave them a look that quieted them instantly. He led Suzy to her chair and pulled it out for her before doing the same for each of the girls. He said the prayer, and they began.

Samuel told the girls he had gotten word the boys were in Utah. "Now, the work begins. They have to do a lot of asking questions and passing out wanted posters. Hopefully, someone soon will have laid eyes on these two. Once they get close enough, they can start tracking."

Willow sighed, "I am so afraid for Lou. I just want him home."

Suzy patted her hand. "We all want them home safe and sound. They have a job to do. Don't fret so, girls. Your men are the best, and they have many friends."

After supper, the girls helped Suzy clean up, so she and Samuel could sit on the porch swing. Samuel loved to put Suzy on his lap and swing with her while they looked at the stars, talking things over while he gently rocked them back and forth. Everyone in the family had found out, at one time or another, it usually ended up with the headboard of their bed hitting the wall later in the night.

Willow and Missy giggled as they heard them talking outside. The girls went to bed early, not wanting to interfere with Suzy and Samuel's alone time. As soon as the girls tiptoed into their room and shut the door, they sat on their beds—they both slept in the same room with twin beds. Willow put on her nightgown and got under the covers first. Missy was not far behind. They waited for a few minutes, and not hearing any sound, they lifted their nightgowns and naughty fingers found their little buds. They both began to rub, being careful not to make too much noise. Willow wet her finger in her own juices and began to circle her little bud harder and faster, until she felt the usual tightening. Both girls covered their faces in the pillows as they lifted their bottoms off the bed in ecstasy when they broke apart within seconds of one another. They giggled as they tiptoed to the basin and quickly cleaned themselves before getting back in bed, turning over, and closing their eyes.

It had been a month, and the girls had not heard a single word from either of their husbands. They asked every ranch hand as they came from town. Nothing! Samuel was busy with everyone else. It was coming on time to start getting ready for the winter. Wood needed to be cut and hauled. Samuel always did his ranch first, and then Hawk and he did the rest of the families', starting with Hawk and Little Bird's home, not far from Samuel's. Next, came the family in town. Shaun and Brenden took care of their own, and they would take care of Lou's and Gabe's as well.

Everyone was working hard. Suzy and the girls were washing all the bedding and either making fresh beds or putting them in the trunks. The garden needed weeding, and the girls were busy making cheeses and wrapping them in wax to keep for the winter. In a few weeks, it would be harvest time, time to harvest the garden and can the vegetables and time to cut the hay. The corn was harvested for the cattle and horses. There were men who ground it and put it in large bags to be stored in the back room in the stable for the horses. Much of it was stored in the back room of the large barn in huge piles for the cattle. The men brought large bags of flour back from the mercantile when they went to town. The pantry was large, but they kept it full at all times.

Suzy did not have an icebox because it was too far from town to have the ice man come, but she had a cold room that Samuel had built in the side of a hill. Inside the room was an artesian well. Samuel had built, with bricks, a round bath where the ice-cold water kept the butter and milk cold all year around. It never froze but was cold all summer.

The girls were getting impatient. Willow wanted to go back to the clinic and her own home and begin getting it ready for the cold winter ahead, and Missy was worried about school and if she would be ready. It was hard to focus on anything but worrying about their husbands.

Spring came to visit, and she brought Anna Mae and the girls dried meat for jerky one day, and the next, Little Bird came, and they got some deer hides ready for her to start making moccasins for everyone. Still, the girls became impatient and moody.

Another week went by, and still no word. The girls' tempers were getting short. They argued amongst themselves and snapped at some of the hands.

One day, Missy made the mistake of snapping at Samuel. He gave her a hard look, shook his head in disbelief and then laid down the law. Samuel's law.

"If you girls don't settle down and stop this childishness, you will feel my strap. You will not disrespect me or my wife and family or my men. Is that understood?"

Missy quickly nodded her head and ran for the house. That settled the girls down for another week, but the week became two, until it was almost two months.

They began planning how to get home. Missy was sure she would not be ready by the time school started, and Willow was afraid Jarod had replaced her.

By the first morning of the second month, the girls had had enough. Samuel was gone for the day helping Brenden and Shaun, and it was just Suzy and the two of them.

"Suzy, we are going home this morning. Enough is enough; we have careers that are suffering."

Suzy shook her head. "No, girls, you will not. Don't you remember when you got married, you promised the men you would obey? Don't you know if they can't trust you to stay with us safely, they can't do their job? If they have to worry about you, it takes their minds off important things like staying safe themselves. You put them in danger when they worry about you instead of their own safety."

Willow felt guilty for just a second before Missy spoke up, "We have worked our entire life for our careers. We cannot stay here any longer. Someone will protect us in town. I know your men are really busy now, but we are going home. Jarod can protect Willow, and the deputy can watch out for me."

The girls started for the door, when Suzy tried one more time. "Girls, please think about what you are doing."

Willow and Missy both turned to her and said, " We are going home now."

Willow shouted, "If you will not loan us a horse, we will walk, but we are going home now." Just as the girls turned for the door again, they ran into a very angry Samuel. He was livid.

"You girls would disrespect my hospitality and sass and yell at my wife. When all we want is to keep you safe?" They turned to Suzy when they heard her sob. They had made Suzy cry. This was not going to end well, and they both knew it.

Samuel walked over to Suzy and held her. He looked over her head at the girls, and they could see the strap very clearly in them. They both were frozen to the floor. Fear made it impossible for them to move.

"You girls go to your room and stay there until I come to get you," he said through clenched teeth. Both girls ran to their room, slamming the door and putting their backs to it, in case Samuel tried to get in. Sliding to the floor, they looked at one another.

"Missy, what are we going to do?"

Missy stared at Willow. "You are the one who yelled at Suzy. You figure out how to get us out of this mess you got us into."

Willow shook her head. "I am not going out there to talk to Samuel."

They moved away from the door, and Missy cracked it enough to see Samuel carrying Suzy toward their room. Shortly after, they heard the front door quietly close.

Missy turned to Willow. "We have to run away. We have to steal a horse and gallop home as fast as we can. Maybe we can stay at the orphanage for a day or two until Samuel cools off."

Willow shook her head frantically and asked, "Are you crazy? He will find us, and he will strap us until there is no skin left. If we run, we are really doomed. No, we have to stay and face the music."

"Oh, God, I am so scared that I can't stay and face the music."

Willow began to sob. "What are we going to do, Missy? Samuel is going to strap us, and it is going to kill us."

Missy stopped and thought for a minute. "I remember Suzy telling me one time, if you wanted to butter up your husband for something, to make him a nice meal. Light candles and make his favorite supper. Compliment him and sit on his lap. We don't have to go that far, for sure, but a nice meal for them both might work. Let's get started before Suzy gets up. It will be a nice surprise."

Willow nodded her head. "Maybe we can apologize nicely and clean up the kitchen and only get a scolding."

She shook her head. "No, he said we would get a strapping, and Samuel never lies. But then again, maybe it won't be a hard one."

Missy cracked open the door and peeked into the living room. All clear.

Both girls quickly and quietly began supper. "Suzy has a nice ham; let's start that. If you want, you can peel the potatoes while I make the biscuits," Willow whispered.

Missy replied, "Why do I always get the dirty jobs? You peel the potatoes."

"Fine, but if Samuel doesn't like your biscuits, it will be your fault if we get a hard strapping."

Missy's eyes got wide. " No," she whispered loudly. "I will peel the potatoes. You know you make the best biscuits, besides Suzy."

Willow found some corn on the cob in the cold room and put the ears in a pot to boil also.

By the time Suzy came out of the bedroom wiping sleep from her eyes, the girls were just setting the table.

Suzy smiled. "This is very nice, girls, but who are you trying to butter up? Me or Samuel?"

Willow replied with a grin, "Both."

"I see, but you know Samuel is pretty immune to being buttered up. He has had me for near on twenty- five years."

Missy spoke right up, "Any suggestions, because he promised us the strap? I know we deserve it, but please help us."

Suzy looked shocked for a second but then shook her head. She shouldn't be surprised; he never could abide anyone making her cry. She tried not to, but she couldn't help it.

"Apologize sweetly is all I can tell you," she said, sympathizing with the girls. She had never had the strap, but Shaun had, once. Thank God, Samuel took him to the woodshed so she didn't hear or see it.

Samuel came in right on time and smiled when he saw the table. Not the food—that, he couldn't care less about, but his wife was smiling and talking to the girls.

"Well, I can see Suzy has told you about buttering the men up. I will have to talk to her about putting ideas in you girls' heads," he teased as he washed up.

Missy and Willow looked at one another before Willow cleared her throat. "About that, sir, we want to apologize for being so rude to you and Suzy. We didn't mean to make Suzy cry. It is just that we have worked so hard all of our lives for our careers and we see them going away. School starts in three weeks, and I am sure Jarod will have replaced me by now and," Willow stumbled, unable to go on for a second before she wailed, " please don't use the strap on us, Samuel. Please, we will do anything you ask, but we are afraid of it."

Missy quickly took over, leading her friend to her chair, "We didn't mean any harm, but our careers are important to us. It has been two months, and we are worried sick about our husbands, too. It is just too much stress." By the time she had finished, she was sobbing, too.

Samuel led her to her chair and sat next to them as Suzy got out his coffee cup and filled it. He sat and watched them until they calmed some. Taking a sip of coffee, he spoke, "I promised the strap, and I never lie. You made my Suzy cry, and there has to be a reckoning for that. I spent the day thinking about it, and I have decided that tomorrow morning, your punishment will begin. You will write one hundred times each, *I will never make Suzy cry again*. Then, you will write another hundred times, *I will never disrespect Samuel again*. After you finish that, you will each get ten stripes with the strap, over your drawers, for sure. The next day, we will all go to town and stay at the hotel until we hear from the boys again." He turned to Missy. "You may get your school things from the mercantile." He then said to Willow, "Jarod can keep an eye on you when you go back to work. You will both stay at the hotel with Suzy and me. Hawk has graciously volunteered to ride with you to the school, Missy. You may thank him later, but thank him, you will."

He sat back into his chair and finished his coffee as the girls quietly got up and dished up supper. After prayer, they all quietly ate. Samuel ate with gusto while Suzy ate slowly, thinking, and the girls picked at their food, dreading the morning.

Finally, Willow said, "Thank you, sir, for taking us home. I only hope you don't spank us too hard." She peeked up at Samuel as she spoke the last sentence.

He only smiled and continued eating without answering her. He helped pick up the plates, as usual, before he sat with another cup of coffee and watched the girls cleaning the kitchen. He pulled Suzy on his lap when she got up to help. When the girls were finished, he told them, "After your punishment, I will be able to tell your husbands I took care of it, when they ask me how you behaved. I will not lie to them."

Willow turned to Samuel, pleading with him, "Please don't tell Lou you had to spank me." She wailed, "They will spank us again. Please do not."

Samuel shook his head. "I will not lie for you. If they ask me, I will tell them. But I will also tell them I took care of it. I can tell them honestly that you will never do it again."

He stood with Suzy in his arms and gave her a sweet kiss. "We are going out on the front porch for a spell. You girls finish up here and go to bed. You will have a big day tomorrow, and you will want to be fresh."

While they were sitting on the swing, Suzy on Samuel's lap, she mused out loud, " Samuel, don't you think the strap is a little too harsh for those little girls?"

Samuel smiled at his beautiful wife. "It's like this, wife. I promised them the strap. I will not break my word, but if you would have asked me before I went out for a ride around the ranch to cool off or before I talked to Hawk, I would have told you that they deserve every bit for making you cry. Now that I cooled off and talked to Hawk and Little Bird, I believe I have mellowed their punishment just right. You see, they are going to worry about it all night. Then, in the morning, they are going to write lines until their fingers want to fall off. By that time, they will be more than willing to get it done and over with. Those ten stripes will not be harsh, but they will be strong enough for them to tell anyone with honesty —anyone who takes a notion to be rude to you, God forbid, to make you cry—that it is very unwise. Understand? I want them to be able to testify to anyone what will happen if they decide to challenge my authority or be rude to you. They will not forget this as long as they live, but because they are getting the extra punishments, I will not have to be as harsh with the strap. Just enough. Along with that, like I said, I will not have to lie to Lou or Gabe. They will not punish the girls again. I will make sure of it."

Suzy put her arms around Samuel's neck and gave him a kiss. "You are so wise, husband. Now, let us go to bed, shall we? I have had a hard day and deserve to be rewarded."

"I agree, wife, we both deserve a reward." He picked her up and headed for their room and paradise.

The girls did not laugh when they heard the headboard bounce against the other wall. They were too worried about their bottoms and the day to come.

The next morning, two girls came out for breakfast with sad faces. Neither of them had gotten much sleep, both of them dreading what was to come.

Suzy smiled at them and served them their rolled oats.

Willow frowned. That was just what she wanted—rolled oats, which she hated, right before a spanking. She pushed her bowl away until she saw the look Suzy gave her. Grabbing her bowl again, she smiled apologetically and began eating her breakfast.

Samuel came in from the woodshed with the strap in his hand.

Both girls swallowed the lump in their throats. It was about an inch wide and a foot and a half long, which did not include the wooden handle, and it was worn from many years of use. Willow gulped again, wondering how many bottoms it had scarred. Maybe even Samuel's.

He laid it on the table between the girls, so they could look at it and dread it even more. "Suzy darlin', will you bring the paper and pencils out here please, for the girls?"

Suzy finished picking up the bowls before she slowly walked into the study for the supplies he had asked for. Placing them on the table, she continued cleaning the kitchen.

"Why don't we leave the girls to do their writing while I help you in the garden?"

"That would be nice, Samuel."

Samuel turned at the back door before he closed it. "You girls have one hour to finish before I start adding stripes."

Willow laid her head on her arms and began crying until she felt Missy hug her.

"Listen, Willow, we have to finish this. Let us get this done so we can get it over with."

Willow looked sadly at her friend before nodding her head. The girls quickly worked to finish the task that Samuel had given them.

Samuel and Suzy returned an hour later, with vegetables to wash and clean for supper, to two very sorry looking girls. Samuel handed the papers to Suzy to look over while he pointed to the empty corner of the living room.

"Stand in the corner, Missy. I will take care of Willow first. Willow, bend over the arm of the couch and lift your dress and petticoats. I want to see your drawers and nothing but."

Willow slowly walked over to the couch and did as she was asked as Samuel went to the table and picked up the strap.

Letting it dangle over Willow's bottom, he began the lecture. "You know why you are here, so let's get to it. I will give you ten stripes each. You may hold the pillow if it helps, because if you put your hands back here, we will start over. If you get out of position, we start over, and after the ten, I will ask Suzy if she found any mistakes in your papers or if they were done sloppily. We will take care of any additional stripes immediately. Do you understand, both of you?"

They both nodded.

"Then let's finish this, and I want you both to know that I have news for you. I will share it with you at supper, tonight."

Samuel positioned Willow so her bottom was where he wanted it and her tiptoes just touched the floor. He picked up the strap and quickly brought it down with a mighty crack on the table in back of the couch, bringing a loud scream from Willow. She jumped up, rubbing her bottom and stomping her feet, going in circles in the hot bottom dance. When she realized that she didn't feel the sting or heat, she looked over to find Samuel leaning against the table with his arms crossed and the strap in his hand. His legs were crossed at the ankles lazily, and he had a huge smile on his face and a twinkle in his eyes. He was laughing at her fright.

Willow's face turned a bright red when she realized what she had done. Slowly, she leaned over the arm again, lifting her clothes one more time as Samuel came back to her.

In a voice that barely hid the laughter, he said, "That one doesn't count."

Willow heard a snicker from the kitchen just as she heard the whistle and felt a strip of fire on her poor bottom.

"Yipes! Ow, please, Samuel, not so hard," she yelled.

Samuel knew he was going very easy on the girls. He didn't need to be harsh. His reputation preceded him. He knew he was giving them no more than a good hand spanking, but the girls were so afraid, even a feather would have brought yells and tears. Willow yelled and sobbed like he had taken a branding iron to her bottom, when, in reality, Suzy and Samuel both knew their bottoms would have a few red stripes but no welts. Sure, they would have problems sitting tomorrow, but they had that coming. Samuel called to Suzy just before the last stripe.

"Is the paper to your satisfaction, wife?"

Suzy called back, "Yes, sir, both of them."

"All right, this is the last one, little one, and it will be the hardest and on the good ole sit spot." With that, he delivered the hardest one of all of them and right where he said he would.

Willow screamed, and Samuel let her up and pulled her into his arms before leading her to the door of her room. He kissed her on the top of her head with a pat on her sore behind before he sent her to her room to lie on her tummy on her bed and cry herself out. Next, came Missy. She got the same treatment and made the same fuss and ended up in the same bedroom on her bed before Samuel turned to Suzy, who nodded her head in agreement.

"Thank you for not being so harsh with them, Samuel. I know they think you are a brute right now, but we both know it was all in their heads. You are a sneaky devil, Samuel, and a sly one." She gave her husband a hug and a kiss before he left for the day. He had news for the girls that would make them happy, but that would have to wait until tonight.

Suzy began a special supper. She knew the news Samuel had, and she knew the girls would be happy to hear it. Tomorrow, early, they would go to town for a spell. She was happy because Little Bird and she had some shopping to do. She also knew the men needed supplies. Samuel needed a new grinding wheel and a new ax.

Brenden and Shaun would be going to town, tomorrow, also. They would all spend the day with family before returning home with much needed supplies. They would make it a nice family day with supper at Kayla's, tomorrow night.

WILLOW AND MISSY stayed in their room. Missy was the first to lift her dress and lower her bloomers to show Willow.

"How does it look, Willow, horrible? Do I have welts?" she sniffed.

Willow looked closely. "No, it is just really red; look at mine. Do I have welts? Am I bleeding?" Willow lowered her boomers for Missy to look.

"No, just really, really red. I think he spanked you harder than me."

"No, I was just being nice. Your bottom is almost purple."

"I thought I saw bruises on your bottom, Willow."

Both girls wiped their eyes and hugged one another.

"Willow, I don't think he spanked us any harder with the strap than our husbands do with their hands."

Willow quickly shook her head. "Shhh, Missy, don't let them hear you say that. He might come in and spank us again. It is best we let them and anyone else who asks think that it really was terrible and horrible."

And *that* is exactly how Samuel's reputation with the strap grew.

After a couple of hours, the girls quietly came out to help Suzy. No one mentioned the spanking. All three of them chatted happily as they all did their share to make Samuel a special meal, with his favorite blueberry pie.

After the table was set and Samuel pulled out the girls' chairs, Willow noticed the pillow on her chair. Samuel must have put it on there when the girls were outside drawing water from the well. She smiled and thanked Samuel kindly.

"How are the bottoms?" he asked.

Willow shook her head. "Oh, they still sting, sir. That strap was so awful."

Missy nodded her head in agreement.

Suzy and Samuel smiled to each other when the girls weren't looking.

Samuel said grace, and everyone ate a delicious meal. Afterwards, the girls all cleaned up, and when they all had a cup of coffee in front of them, Samuel began.

"I have some good news and some bad. First, your husbands should be home by tomorrow night or the next morning. The bad news is they didn't get the men, so you still have to have a chaperone."

Willow squealed with delight, "Lou is coming home. I am so happy."

Missy looked at Samuel before she said quietly, "Samuel, are you sure they won't spank us again?"

"I gave you my word, Missy. Would I lie to you?"

"No, sir, but our husbands have a mind of their own, and they are in charge of us."

"I will talk to them; don't fret on it. I want you to pack all your things tonight, so we can leave at first light. I have a lot to do when I am in town, so it isn't a wasted trip."

Both girls finished their coffee and ran to their room. They were going home!

A SURPRISE

Before dawn, they loaded the wagons and started for town. Little Bird and Hawk took Willow, and Samuel and Suzy took Missy. The hard bench made it hard to sit still and it was a very long way to town. Suzy had asked Samuel if she could provide pillows for the girls, but he nixed the idea.

"Lou and Gabe will want proof the girls were punished sufficiently. I want a little pink left, at least, or my reputation will be shot." He chuckled.

Suzy smiled at her husband of many years. He never failed to surprise her.

The girls were very happy, but by late morning, they were glad to arrive and to be able to get down. Samuel gave them strict orders not to leave the hotel until either he or Hawk could go with them. The girls each unpacked a dress for their supper at Kayla's.

Missy was making a list of things she needed at the mercantile for school and some of the things she had to be picked up. "The chalk and the slates should be in and maybe some of the new books I had ordered," she thought out loud.

Willow was anxious to see Jarod. "I wonder how ole mister Wilson is doing. He broke his foot. The last I saw him, he was recovering pretty well, but you never know. He was my favorite. Did I tell you Jarod gave him a job? Poor ole guy has not been the same since he lost Matilda. Jarod lets him sweep up and dump the garbage," she babbled happily.

Suzy and Little Bird just nodded good naturedly while listening to the girls' chatter.

There was a knock on the door, and when Suzy answered it, there stood Shaun and Anna Mae and Brenden and Spring.

Spring gave Willow and Missy both a hug before she took Missy's hand. "Brenden and I have volunteered to take you to the mercantile and then to the school. Come on, Missy. I will help you clean and air the school out."

Anna Mae then said to Willow, " Come on, girl. Shaun and I will take you to the clinic and then to your home to get it aired out and ready for your man. I bought a chocolate cake at the new bakery just next to the hotel. We can have dessert when we are finished."

Willow laughed gaily as she walked along with her friends. The first stop was the clinic. She was so happy that the first person she saw was Mr. Wilson.

"Mr. Wilson, how are you?" she asked.

"Just fine, Willow. Jarod is taking the wrapping off my foot for good, soon. I will see how the foot works, then. I haven't been able to walk to the cemetery since my accident. I miss my visits with Matilda."

Willow nodded her head in understanding. Patting him on the back, she went in search of Jarod. He was in the back room taking inventory of the medicines. When he looked up, he smiled brightly.

"Willow, how good it is to see you back. Are you ready to come back to work?"

"I am so happy you are willing to keep me on, what with having to leave on such short notice."

"You are family, Willow. I could never replace you. We all love you. Now, do you want to help me with your favorite patient? I think we have kept Mr. Wilson waiting long enough."

While Shaun and Anna Mae waited, Willow helped Jarod take the bandages off.

"I am very pleased, Roger. I think we can leave the bandage off, but I would warn you not to overdo it."

Roger Wilson looked at Jarod sadly. "I have to get to the cemetery to visit Matilda. She is probably lonely by now."

Jarod shook his head. "I don't want you doing too much on the foot yet. I tell you what; we don't have any more patients today. How about I take you to the cemetery? I'll lock up, and we will be ready to go, but I want you to promise to stay and guard the clinic at night. You can sleep in the spare room in back. I don't want you to go all the way out to the farm yet. Is that all right with you? In return for your guarding services, I will take you to the cemetery whenever you want. Is it a deal?" Jarod held out his hand, and Roger took it gratefully.

"You bet, Jarod; I will guard the clinic at night really good."

Willow smiled at Jarod. She loved him for his patience and soft heart. She knew no one ever bothered the clinic. No one dared give Samuel's family any trouble.

Willow walked out into the waiting room to find Anna Mae and Shaun waiting patiently. They went just a few houses down from the clinic, past Jarod and Autumn's house, to Willow and Lou's comfortable home. When they entered, they saw that Autumn had stocked the icebox and there was a fresh block of ice in it, as well as a few groceries, like milk and cheese and butter. The house smelled stuffy and stale, so the girls opened the windows while Shaun brought in enough wood for a couple of nights. The days still were warm, but the nights were becoming colder.

Willow wanted to wash the bedding and hang it out but not today. Today was just getting ready for Lou to come home. The girls went out back and picked some flowers for the table.

Anna Mae pointed to the garden. "One of the girls has been weeding for you while you were gone. That is really nice of them."

"Yes, we will probably be having our canning party soon. I think it is at Autumn's this year."

Anna Mae smiled. "This year is my mom's year to have a canning party. I do Shaun's family one year, and mine the next. Suzy invited my family to our Christmas this year, too. I am excited to have everyone meet them."

"Suzy always has room in her heart for more family. Have no fear; they will fit right in."

Anna Mae put her arm around Willow as they headed back into the house with their flowers for the table. Shaun had just made coffee and had the cake out on the table. Willow got out the plates and forks, and the three of them sat down for a nice snack and a chat.

Shaun brought the forbidden topic up first, "I heard Missy tell Brenden you two got Samuel's strap."

Willow's face turned bright red. "Yes," she said. "We made your ma cry with sassin' her to come home."

Shaun looked in disbelief. "You made Ma cry and Pa saw it?"

Anna Mae looked from one to the other. "Well, spill it. What happened?"

Willow looked down at her cake. Somehow, she had lost her appetite thinking about what a terrible person she was to make Suzy cry.

Shaun gave her a jab with his elbow. " I got the strap one time for not putting on my pistol before I went out to the fence line. Pa sent me to the woodshed, so Ma wouldn't have to see. I thought he tore the hide off my butt."

Anna Mae's eyes got wide. "Oh, my."

Willow put her fork down as she began her story, " We were so afraid our jobs were over because Lou and Gabe sent us for two months out in the country. We had worked our tails off to build our careers. Well, after two months, we had enough, so Missy and I decided we would disobey Samuel and go home, whether he liked it or not. Suzy tried to reason with us, but I yelled at her. She began to cry, and when we turned to go out the door, Samuel was standing in it looking like he wanted to strangle us. God, Shaun," she looked at both of them, " I feel so bad that I made her cry. The strap hurt so bad, I thought I was gonna die."

Shaun nodded his head. "Oh, how I know."

Anna Mae looked at both of them before her small voice filled with fear. "I don't ever want the strap. Nope. I will never make Suzy cry. Not one time."

Shaun laughed. "You are so good. I never even have to spank you."

Anna Mae got a stubborn look in her eye. "I am naughty, sometimes, hoping you care enough to take me in hand, but you never do." She put her hands over her face and began to sob softly.

Shaun looked up at Willow, confused, his eyes asking her what he should do.

Willow put her plate and cup in the sink while Shaun tried to talk to Anna Mae. "I am going to see if there are some fresh vegetables for supper tomorrow night."

Shaun held his wife as she sniffed back her sorrow. "I am sorry, Shaun. I know the rest of the family practices domestic discipline. I see how they never fight or argue. Not saying we do over much, but I want what everyone else has."

Shaun was in shock for a second. He never realized. "If that is what you want, then we will try it. I just thought your feelings get hurt so easily that I didn't need to take that hard of a stand. I didn't realize you felt this way. We will sit down when we get home and discuss some rules, in that case."

Anna Mae nodded against his chest, and he kissed the top of her head. "I love you, Anna, don't ever forget it. If you need something from me, you need to tell me. Since you kept this from me and gave me no chance to correct things, I think you deserve a spanking when we get home."

Again, she nodded her acceptance.

Willow came in whistling to give the couple inside a heads-up.

Anna Mae boasted, "Shaun is going to spank me tomorrow."

Willow laughed as she put the vegetables in the sink. "Whatever, little sister, whatever."

Shaun shook his head and laughed. "We should begin to get ready for supper, so why don't we head back to the hotel?"

Willow agreed and ran to get her pretty yellow dress, the one Lou liked so much. She was hoping he would come home tonight. She missed him so much.

As they walked down the boardwalk chatting away, Willow noticed the light on at the office. Her eyes lit up. "Shaun, the men are home. The lights are on at the office. Hurry, come on." She took Anna Mae's hand and began dragging her in the direction of the office just as Gabe came out from the stable. Willow gave a scream, and Gabe turned and waved to her as he headed back inside the office.

Lou came out and looked down the road at his little sprite running, dragging Anna with her. A weary smile crossed his face.

Willow could see it was her big husband silhouetted in the doorway. The light shining behind him, he filled the entire door. She squealed again, but this time, Anna disentangled her hand and let her run. Lou stepped down to meet her and pulled her up off her feet as he kissed her. Her feet in the air, he turned her around and around, never letting go of her lips.

"Oh, Lou, I have missed you so much."

He set her on the ground, giving her another quick kiss as he held out his hand to shake Shaun's outstretched one and bent down to give Anna a kiss on the cheek.

"I stopped to let Samuel know we're back. He is making sure the family is all gathered for supper. We have bad news, but we also have a surprise."

He looked at Willow just as he heard a squeal coming from further down the road.

"Seems Missy has seen us, too. I am going to change and will meet you at Kayla's, little one. I need a wash, too." He gave Shaun a nod and Willow a pat on the bottom before he turned to go back into the office.

"Let's hurry and get ready, " an excited Willow said as she danced around. The girls laughed gaily as Shaun led them to the hotel.

∼

WILLOW PUT on her pretty yellow dress and took care with her hair. Suzy gave her a pretty yellow ribbon and weaved it into her braid before she wound some of it around her head and left the rest of her hair to hang down to her waist.

The family was all gathering, just as Lou and Gabe entered the restaurant.

Willow looked at her husband in the gaslight. He looked exhausted. She promised herself that when she got him home, she would pamper him with a hot bath and hot sex before they went to sleep. Not necessarily in that order. She smiled as he sat next to her and took her small hand in his large, rough one.

"Let's enjoy a good meal and loving family before we get to the discussions," Samuel began. He wanted everyone to enjoy the night first, before he let the girls know the restrictions still held.

Kayla pulled up a chair and sat with the family tonight, also. She needed to tell Tom what was going on, and the wait staff was perfectly capable of handling the dinner crowd.

After a lovely meal, Lou pushed his chair back some, patting his stomach. "Kayla, this restaurant is still one of the very best in Buffalo." Everyone agreed.

Lou began, in a slow but clear voice. This was too important. "We lost Willard and Terry. They killed a ferry driver and his family and loaded the horses, floating away on the ferry. We don't know where they got off. The ferry was cut loose and left floating down the river. We decided to come home and leave some of our Pinkerton friends to keep searching. One of the barkeeps remembers them coming in and having a few drinks before they left town again." Lou looked at Willow as he said, "One of them mentioned to the barkeep that he was going to see his sisters, Willow and Missy." Lou watched as the girls' eyes grew in fear. "He knew we would end up at that bar and he knew the barkeep would tell us what he said. They know who you are, and they are toying with us, letting us know they are coming for you girls."

Gabe stood up, stalking back and forth as he added, "We would like to send you girls away to Boston, to Jarod's sister's home for a short while, until we can catch these men." He looked at his Missy with sadness in his eyes.

Willow and Missy both stood, and Missy exclaimed, "No! Enough is enough. We both have careers. It is not fair of you to ask us to leave again." Missy stomped her foot and crossed her arms over her chest. Both girls were ready for battle.

Willow shouted to Lou, "We are *not* leaving, and that is final. You men figure out how to protect us, but our families are here, and, here, we will stay safe."

The other diners looked on as the two girls stood firm.

Samuel began to say, "You girls could—"

Willow and Missy shook their heads emphatically. "No!" they both shouted.

Lou looked sternly at Willow. "You will do as you are told. These men are psychopaths; they enjoy causing pain, watching others suffer it. They have no conscience or guilt or remorse. They are the sneakiest and slyest men I have ever dealt with, cunning and manipulative to the extreme. I want you all in this family to know this. We will allow you to stay, but only because Gabe and I have brought home some help. I still don't like it, but it will have to do for now."

Gabe looked at the rest of the women. "Under no circumstances, for any reason whatsoever, are any of you to go out alone. This is the most danger you have ever been in. I am sorry we brought it home, but there is no help for it. I suspect they will be here soon, if they are not already. Missy, the deputy is willing to escort you to school and back and stay while you teach. The sheriff has hired a deputy just for you. You will obey him in all things. The sheriff has a son in your class, and he has asked that Samuel provide men to make rounds guarding the school and protecting the children. The school is right in town; it should not be difficult for us to keep an eye on it and the children as they come and go. We don't want the townspeople to find out about this and start a panic, but they need to know these men are dangerous. We will hold a town meeting and hand out flyers with the men's pictures. The deputies will go around talking to farmers, in case they see something. Lou and I are going to talk to Ada at the Crooked Antler, to ask her to talk to her girls and to ask them to keep a watch out. And, under no circumstances, are they to go alone with one of these men. I will do that, tonight, before I go home. I have a friend at the house who will be staying for a while."

He turned to Samuel, then. " We have brought Ben Carson home with us. He has gifts for the girls."

Samuel finally understood. " I understand. I have known Ben for many years. He is a good man, worked for the Pinkertons for many years. I assume he will stay with Missy while you go to the Crooked Antler."

"Yes, and now, it has been a hell of a couple of months. I know I would like to be done for the night. I would like you all to come with us to the stable, so I can introduce you all to the girls' surprise."

Everyone got up and followed the boys out to the stable, including Kayla.

As Gabe opened the door, out ran two German Shepherd pups. Both appeared to be about six months old and good sized pups, already.

Lou called Willow's to him, "Major, come. Sit." The dog was very obedient.

Gabe did the same for Missy's dog. "Starla, come. Sit."

Willow stood still, letting the pup smell her hands and feet. The dogs already were half way to the girls' waists.

Major lifted his paw for Willow to take, and when she did, the dog looked into her eyes with his soft brown ones and Lou knew they would have no problem bonding.

Willow began to rub him behind his ears as she spoke softly to him about what a beautiful dog he was. Major began to wag his tail and whine, looking to Lou.

"I have not released him yet, Willow." He bent down and whispered the word, "Release."

Major immediately barked and stood so Willow could pet him easier. His tail wagging mightily, he nuzzled his nose into Willow's hand, barking for attention.

Willow giggled. "I love my puppy."

"These dogs are trained to protect," Ben said as he walked into the barn, bringing the mood back to somber. "They come from two different bitches, so you can mate them and train them, which is what I plan to do with my two. I have two out back that are small yet and being trained. I will sell them later. These dogs have to bond with the girls. I need you to take them home with you and let them get to know you. In one week, we will begin their training. They will be trained to protect you with their lives, and, girls," he looked at both of them, "these dogs will kill for you at your command if the situation warrants it."

Willow nervously twisted her dress. "But I work at the clinic; how can he follow me to work?"

Ben looked to Jarod, before he turned back to Willow. "You will tell him to guard. He will lie in front of the door and will not move until you release him. He is already trained to do that. He will, on his own, lie by your door, but he will only stay and not wander if you tell him to guard. It will protect the patients, also, in case one of these men come for an unexpected visit. You must remember to release him to go out the back to do his duty and to feed and water him."

Jarod looked doubtful. "I don't know about this. What if he bites one of the children?"

"Major or Starla will never attack or bite without Willow or Missy's directed instruction. Give it a try."

Jarod still looked doubtful but reluctantly agreed, "We will try it, Willow. If it doesn't work, it doesn't." He turned to Lou. "You act like I can't protect my family, and I take offense to that. I have a rifle in my office and a handgun," he said angrily.

Lou wanted to sooth his ruffled feathers. "I know you can protect your family, but these men will not give you time to get your gun. They will snatch Willow in a heartbeat, and, Jarod," he stopped for emphasis, "if they take one of the girls, they will torture them. They will not care how much pain they cause them. They are psychopaths, they enjoy hurting others. They will especially like hurting *these* girls. We put them in prison; they would love to cause us all kinds of hell."

Jarod looked at Lou, seeing the torment he was feeling just thinking about it.

"All right, I will give it a try."

Ben spoke up again, " I will see you girls in one week's time. You are all welcome to watch the training. In fact, I encourage it."

THE PUP

"Let's go home, little one, I have had no sleep and less food in the last couple of days, trying to hurry home to you." To Major, he ordered, "Heel."

The dog followed close behind them both, to the amazement of everyone but Ben and Gabe. Once they arrived, Lou unlocked the door and entered first, leaving Willow and Major just inside the door while he went through every room to make sure it was secure. When he was satisfied, he turned on the gaslights.

"I am glad the town council approved a streetlight outside our door. It is smart that they put one outside of the sheriff's office and our office, too, but most importantly, outside the Crooked Antler Saloon." He put a few logs in both fireplaces while Willow sat on the bed and took down her beautiful hair.

Lou stood from lighting the fire and turned to look at his beautiful wife. Her wheat-colored hair floated past her waist as she untangled the braids. She smelled of outside and fresh air. As the dress fell to her feet, his cock twitched and became a steel rod instantly. He walked over to her and plucked at her pert breasts. Not too big and not too small. Just the right size. She moaned as he again plucked at her nipples, making them pebble. Lou took her in his arms and lifted her, so she straddled his waist. He reached down to release his cock and guided it into her weeping channel. Slowly, he pumped into her until she threw her head back, her hair tickling his knees as he did the dance of a man and a woman, slowly and gently, even though it took all he had not to pound into her and find his release. *No*, she had waited for him, also. He could feel her clamp down on him just as he felt his release. Together, they broke apart, finding their piece of heaven. He lowered her and retrieved the washcloth to clean them. He kissed her forehead as he brought her to his chest.

"I need to go and get the dog food. Ben should have left it by now at the front door. You put on that pretty see-through nighty you bought and wait for me while I take care of Major."

Lou went to retrieve the hundred-pound bag of dog food. Next, he found two large bowls, one for food and one for water. He put them next to the back door.

He grabbed an old blanket and folded it, putting it on the floor just outside their bedroom door for the dog's bed, then he let Major outside the back door to do his business for the night. Major came in and wearily lay on his bed, his head on his paws looking up at Lou.

"I know, boy, we have all had a hell of a couple of months. You sleep now. I will see you in the morning." He rubbed him behind the ears for a few seconds before turning toward his room.

He saw his wife in her gorgeous yellow silk nighty. The light behind her allowed him to see everything underneath—her pert breasts and rosy colored nipples, the neatly trimmed hair at the junction of paradise. Her legs, although short, were shapely and strong. He twirled his fingers in a circular motion and Willow obediently turned, showing him her cute little bottom before she turned back to face him.

"I don't know why I have you put this on. I just take it right off, but, darlin', the sight of it on you makes me so hard it hurts." Lou chuckled. He walked to her and gently lifted it up, but before it cleared her head, he bent down and took a nipple in his mouth, gently sucking.

Willow moaned, rubbing her legs together to sooth the tingle.

Lou finished lifting the delicate gown off and neatly put in on the dresser. He turned back to her and lifted her to the bed. It had been so damn long for both of them.

He crawled in and nibbled on her neck before he returned to her nipples. Plucking and twisting one and sucking on the other, his teeth gently scraping as he pulled. His hand found her soaking pussy. Inserting first one and then two fingers, he could feel her heat. Her pussy clamped down on his fingers as he went in and out. Her bottom lifted off the bed to meet his fingers.

"God, Lou, please! I can't stand it. Please give me what I need." She knew he would ask, so she finished, "I need your cock inside of me. Please, Lou, let us try and make a baby, tonight."

Lou just chuckled. "I lead the dance, little one, now roll over for your spanking. Have you been a good girl or a bad girl?"

"Oh, please, Lou, you know. I know Samuel told you he spanked us with the strap. We have been punished enough. Please, aww! Please."

Lou laughed again. "Besides that, little one. We will forget that incident. Did you help Suzy the rest of the time? Were you good girls?"

"Yesssss, Lou, we were very good."

He rolled her over onto her stomach and gave her a light smack, just enough to warm her bottom. The warmth would spread to other parts of her body, further down. As he continued to smack and rub, Willow began to twist back and forth, lifting her bottom as if asking for more. The slight sting began a fire in her woman parts —something Willow often wondered about.

Once she began to moan, he turned her over again and knelt before her open legs. Placing his rock-hard cock at her entrance, he impaled her to the hilt. He threw back his head and let out a moan as he rocked in and out, pounding faster and harder until Willow screamed out his name as she again reached for the stars. Lou was right behind her, roaring out his own release. He continued pumping until every drop was gone before he pulled out and pulled her into his strong arms. He kissed the top of her head. "Look at the door." Just outside the door, with just his nose stuck in, barely able to see, was Major.

"He is sneaking a peek to make sure we are all right." Willow heard the rumble of laughter as she lay on his chest.

"Go to sleep, boy. Everything is fine," Lou reassured the dog as he got up for the cloth again. He crawled back in, pulling Willow back into his arms, and they both fell asleep.

The next morning, Lou rolled over, finding the other side of the bed warm but empty. The smell of pancakes and bacon brought a smile to his lips. He found his pants and quickly put them on, coming out to the kitchen without his shirt.

Willow smiled as she looked at her husband. He was such a handsome man. The dark hair on his chest traveled to his waist. Her gaze then went to the muscular arms she loved so much. Strong enough to hold her with no problems, but he tempered that strength when she had a spanking coming. He never spanked her more than she could bear, always just enough to get his point across. His hands were large and strong, like the rest of him. At six-foot-five, he was big enough to keep her safe. Many men feared him. His dark brown eyes could be very cold. She only knew the love in them. Many of the women around town hated her for taking him off the market.

"Are you done looking, darlin'? I am hungry as a bear. First, I will let Major out to do his duty. That will be your job, from now on. I will also show you how to feed him. I want you to do that, also. I want him to know it is you who cares for him. I want you to spend every minute you can with him. Bond with him, so he knows he needs to protect you."

He finished with Major just as the bacon was fried to perfection. He helped Willow set the table, pulled out her chair and said a quick prayer before he dug in. His eyes rolled as he tasted the light pancakes.

"Darlin', you are the best cook in these parts. It sure beats camp food."

Willow smiled at the compliment. She had worked hard, learning from Suzy many recipes. She'd paid attention to what Lou liked and disliked.

"I will walk you to the clinic this morning. I want you to wait for me to come and get you tonight. If I don't come when you close, please go home with Jarod until I can get away. Do you understand, Willow?"

Willow nodded her head in agreement. She didn't like being tied down any more than the other women did, but if it kept her in town and not at the ranch, she would gladly comply.

"If I find out you are going out on your own, it will mean a hard spanking, Willow. You are not ready to be alone, even with Major. He has not been completely trained yet."

Willow sighed, "I know, Lou. I understand. I will take a blanket for Major, so he can lie next to the door. We will see how he does in the clinic."

As Jarod followed behind Willow and Lou, the dog obediently followed behind Willow. Lou helped Willow put the blanket on the floor beside the door and watched as Willow gave the guard order. Major immediately lay on the bed.

"Remember when you take time for lunch to let him outside. Give him some extra time to get some exercise. Make sure you feed and water him."

"I will, Lou, I promise." She bent down to give Major a rub behind the ears. Jarod bent down and petted the dog after Willow did.

∽

THE CLINIC WAS full of women and babies. Willow and Jarod were both impressed at how well-behaved Major was. He lay quietly, not bothering anyone. He just watched the door and, occasionally, the children. Today, Malissa and Mary were in the waiting room with their sons, Luke and Avery, both a year old. Some of the miners had come in for a checkup, and two of the ranchers sat in the waiting room. Suddenly, Willow and Jarod heard Major whining. Willow went out to check on him and found Luke and Avery poking him and pulling his ears. The dog didn't move, except to whine. Willow looked over at Malissa and Mary, who were gossiping about some poor girl in town.

"You women need to keep a better eye on your children," Willow scolded as Jarod came out and took in what was happening.

"You should not have a dog in the clinic if he will bite. Dirty animals do not belong in here," Malissa complained. " Don't you agree, Mary? We can take our business elsewhere."

Jarod spoke up angrily, "You two women need to keep an eye on your children. There are quite a bit of dangerous things here that could hurt them."

"Well, I never! Mary, let us leave here. We don't need to do business here."

One of the ranchers stood up to the snooty Malissa, "You have been bad mouthing Molly since you got in here, woman. I, for one, am sick and tired of listening to you girls gossiping about everyone in town. Instead of gossiping, you should be watching your children." He turned to Jarod. "I am going to find Sonny and Harold and tell them exactly what their wives have been up to." With that, Arnold left in a huff to find Sonny and Harold while the women stood dumbfounded. After a second's hesitation, both women gathered their children and left.

Willow said, "I am so sorry, Jarod."

Jarod replied, "The dog was not at fault."

All of the men left in the waiting room quickly agreed, which left Willow feeling better.

That night, as she walked home with Lou, she explained what happened at the clinic. He just shook his head.

"Harold is the head of the bank on the other side of town. It has struggled mightily, and those women and their gossip haven't helped Harold one bit. As for Sonny, he owns the shoe shop, and his business has fallen in the last year, also. Just about the time Mary started hanging around with Malissa."

The next morning, as Lou walked Willow to the clinic, he reminded her to bring Major to the office. "Ben wants to begin training Major and Starla to defend you." To Jarod, he added, "You and the rest of the family are invited to attend if you're interested. Samuel and Hawk will also be there."

Jarod agreed to pass the word to the rest of the family.

Before they could get organized for the day, Sonny and Harold and their wives and children came in. Jarod looked at the men. Neither looked happy as Harold gave Malissa a slight nudge towards Willow and Jarod.

"Well, wife, what have you to say?"

Malissa licked her lips, looking down at her shoes first before looking at Willow and Jarod.

"I am truly sorry for how I behaved yesterday. Harold, um, has explained to me how rude I was." She looked at Willow. "You were right. I should have watched Luke better. He could have been bitten. I should have taken the opportunity to teach him how to behave around animals."

Both Willow and Jarod accepted her apology, and before they could turn around, Sonny stepped forward. "Doc, please don't take it out on our children because their mas are rude. Arnold told us what was going on, and I guess we both knew it, but it was just so easy to ignore and not have to deal with it. I have talked to Harold, and we both spanked the daylights out of these girls. Should have taken them in hand earlier. Please let the boys continue coming to this clinic."

Mary stepped forward, tears glistening in her eyes. "We are

really sorry. We both have promised our husbands no more gossiping."

Sonny added, "I have forbidden Mary from seeing Malissa until I know she has changed. I have seen a change come over Mary I didn't like, after she became friends with her."

Malissa cried out loud, "Please, Sonny, don't take away the only friend I have."

Sonny shook his head, looking at Harold.

"You brought this on yourself, wife," was Harold's only comment. Malissa began to cry as Harold led her to the chair. He sat next to her to await their turn to take little Luke in to see the doctor. Sonny and Mary sat on the other side of the clinic waiting room with Avery. Mary took the time to lead Avery over to Major and show him how to pet the doggy, talking softly to Major while her son petted him.

Willow noticed both girls sat carefully on the padded chairs, and it brought a grin to her face.

Jarod brought out Avery to a very happy Mary. "Your son is in fine health, Mary, and thank you for showing him how to properly pet a dog and talk to one. Make sure he knows, also, that not all dogs are friendly. He needs to ask permission, first."

Jarod had asked that the men come with their sons in the examining room, leaving the women in the waiting room to talk. He explained to the men the reason that Major was at the clinic in the first place. He told them the dog not only protected Willow but everyone who came into the clinic. Both men understood and agreed to keep a close eye out for the Rose brothers.

After Willow let Major out and she fed him, she walked with him and Jarod to the office, where Ben was waiting for them. Ben asked Missy and Willow to bring their dogs off to the side and have them sit next to them until he called them.

The girls saw the men dressing up in funny looking suits—padded all around in thick jackets up past their ears and pants. Lou put on a facemask made of small wire bars across his face. Willow looked on, curious as to what was going on.

Ben called her over first, "Stand here with Major. Lou, go further out and start coming towards Willow.

As she watched Lou come towards her in a threatening manner, Ben bent down to her ear and whispered, "Call out "sic 'em" as loud as you can."

Willow looked at him in confusion until Ben repeated what he had just said.

"Sic 'em, Major!" she called, and the dog instantly transformed from the loving dog she knew to a growling, barking, angry dog. He ran to Lou and jumped on him, almost knocking him down. Growling and barking, he began tearing at Lou's protective suit, shaking his head. Lou put his arm up to protect himself, but the dog was everywhere, tearing and trying to get at the big man.

Willow cried out, "Major, stop, leave him alone." She was terrified for her husband. As the dog stopped, she cried out and ran to Lou, hugging him. Lou held her for a few minutes before he took off his suit. She was shaking and crying so hard, he couldn't understand her. He picked her up and held her like a child as she wrapped her arms around his neck and her legs around his waist.

With his arms under her bottom, he gently patted it, crooning woods of comfort, "It is all right, Willow. This is practice. I was padded; he couldn't hurt me."

Willow laid her head on his shoulder as he continued to pat her back and bottom.

Missy's eyes were wide with fright. "I will not say it; I will not. Gabe, you take that off right now. I will not do it."

Ben sighed, "Missy, this is for your own good. We must train the dog to protect you. If someone came to harm you or Willow, that is what he would face. With no protective gear, the dog will kill anyone you tell her to. She will protect you against anyone who tries to harm you."

Gabe glanced at Missy before he put the facemask on. Then, he said, "You will do as you are told, Missy, or suffer the consequences. I don't want to spank you today, but I most certainly will if you force me. Now, do what Ben tells you." He put on the facemask and squatted down, ready to take the weight of the dog.

Missy said the words in a whisper, but the dog took off on a run and repeated what Major had done.

Ben bent down to Missy and whispered, "Tell her to stop. Starla, stop."

Missy said the words that made her dog become the loving pup she grew to love again.

Lou let Willow down and took her by the hand to Jarod. Major was wagging his tail and following behind them.

Jarod's face was white with shock at seeing exactly what the dogs were capable of.

"I am now afraid to have Major in the clinic. Is that what you wanted, Lou?"

"No, Jarod. Major will not hurt anyone unless Willow is in danger, and then, only if she tells him to. He will obey her, whether she tells him to lie down or to kill. That is how he will protect her. We have to practice twice a week, so you girls may as well get used to it. After a couple of weeks, we will only have to practice once a month. Not just to attack but how to obey every order."

The next day at the clinic, Willow again heard Major whining. This time, he came to the door and barked and then went back to the waiting room and whined. As Willow and Jarod came out, they could hear laughter.

Major had a little girl by the back of the dress. She was crawling towards the door and Major was trying to stop her. He turned to go back to the door and bark, but he saw Willow standing there with a smile on her face. He went back and lay in front of the child, licking her face, trying to stop her from crawling closer to the door. The child giggled as the dog licked her face, laughing out loud. The rest of the waiting room looked on, laughing too. Major went behind the child and pulled her little dress to pull her back. Willow and

Jarod stood in the doorway laughing until they both held their stomachs, right along with everyone else. Maggie finally picked up her daughter.

"That dog is the best dog I have ever seen. He protected my Sue from going out the door. He is one smart dog." She bent down to pet Major and rub his ears. "He deserves a treat," she declared, and everyone agreed. Everyone pitched in a penny for a real bed for the dog, so he could lie in comfort next to the door. Willow gladly accepted with a pride-swelled heart. After that, word got around, and everyone loved Major and asked after him if he was not in his usual place, for some reason. Mr. Wilson occasionally took him for a walk to the graveyard to visit Matilda. It gave them both much-needed exercise. Mr. Wilson spent many nights sleeping at the clinic. In an emergency, he came to get Jarod lickity-split. It saved Roger a walk to the other side of town and an empty house.

WINTER'S COMING

The men had been home a month, and the days were getting colder. Everyone started thinking of winter. The men were getting hay for the stable and buying grain to fill the bins, enough to last through the frigid months. The women were getting ready for their annual canning party. The men would stay busy and out of their hair getting ready for their own winter chores. Lou and Willow invited Missy and Gabe over for breakfast one morning to discuss what needed to be done yet. Samuel and Hawk stopped in for coffee after their breakfast.

"We need to get Mica over here to clean the chimneys," Lou began.

Gabe added, "We need more wood, and I need to repair the meat locker out back."

Samuel looked up from his cup. "The girls are going to be at Autumn's for two days, canning, so we can haul the wood then. If you men want to come back to the ranch and load up some wood to bring it back, it would save time. I have the sheriff watching Autumn's house while the girls are canning. That frees us up to take care of business. Also, Hawk is going to be coming and going, hanging around the girls.

Something was bothering Samuel. Lou could tell by the way he kept looking into his cup.

Finally, he looked up at the men and said, " I don't know why we haven't heard a peep from the Rose brothers. It has been a month. It worries me, which is why Hawk is going to be staying with Ben."

All the men agreed it was odd and that they needed to be extra vigilant.

Lou said, "I will talk to Mica. If he can do the families' chimneys, that would be great. Tom and Storm and Mark will need theirs done, also. We will schedule him to do Autumn's as soon as the girls are done with the canning."

Gabe got up from the table and held his hand out to Missy. "I'll help Missy get the vegetables and apples ready to take to Autumn's, and then we can hook up the team and help Samuel haul wood for everyone. With two wagons and the Clydesdales, we should have plenty of wood for everyone in no time."

Samuel stood and walked to the door. "Then, we can work on the meat lockers and secure them, so animals don't get into our meat this winter. Brenden will bring the girls and their goods back with him when he comes to town, tomorrow. He has his own wood to cut and things that need to be done for his ranch hands and his family. He will not be staying but will return in two days when the girls are done. Jennifer has volunteered to watch the children while the girls work, and in return, the girls are giving them canned goods. I will talk to Hawk and meet you here in an hour."

Willow began finding all the baskets to put the vegetables into. Autumn had a shed out back that the girls could put their vegetables and fruits into. They brought one vegetable at a time into the house, canned it all and then went on to the next. Missy had the best apples and strawberries, while Willow grew the best pears, corn and beans. Every family grew a field of one or two vegetables and they pooled them all together and divided the canned goods at the end of the canning party. Everyone brought enough jars for their family, along with lids and rings. The girls spent two days working hard, but they had so much fun. They discussed things near to their hearts and traded recipes. Usually, one or two of them had new canning ideas. This year, Suzy found a new recipe from one of the church ladies—apple pie in a jar. She claimed that one made the apple pie filling and canned it, so whenever she wanted to make an apple pie, she just opened a jar and filled the crust. The girls enjoyed the *girl time* and enjoyed a little time to themselves. They knew the men had their own things to do to get ready for winter. Winters were harsh and early.

Willow was so excited by the time suppertime arrived, she could not sit still. Lou had made it back with one load of wood and was dirty and tired. He ate while Willow filled the tub.

She went back to check on him and found him sound asleep in the bed. She smiled and crawled in behind him.

The next morning, Lou was up and making breakfast before Willow woke up. The smell of bacon enticed her into opening her eyes. As she slid into one of her older work dresses, she could hear Lou letting Major out. She heard the plates being placed on the table and could smell the coffee brewing. She slipped into her shoes and smiled as she put her arms around her husband.

"Is there anything that smells as good as coffee in the morning?"

Lou looked down into her eyes before he bent to give her a kiss. "Let Major in, will you?"

After they cleaned the kitchen, Lou helped her gather all her jars and vegetables and helped her take them out back into Autumn's shed. He bent down and gave her another kiss before he patted her bottom.

"We will meet at Kayla's for supper, tomorrow night. Until then, we men will try and disturb you as little as possible. I am going with Samuel to get more wood for Mark and Jarod. I know you all sleep at Autumn's, so we will stay at the office or the hotel. If you need us, that is where we will be."

Willow smiled as she and Major entered Autumn's home. Everyone was already there sipping coffee. Wynter was huge and would be little help, but it was nice to have her there to talk to and it was easier to guard her when the women were all together. It left the men free to do what needed to be done.

Hawk was in and out, keeping an eye on things and helping when he could, carrying in boxes of vegetables and jars. Ben and he took turns taking the younger dogs out back as part of their training. From time to time, Hawk took Major or Starla out for walks.

Wynter stayed busy making a big kettle of soup thick with meat and vegetables. It hung on a hook near a low fire. Everyone ate as they had time.

By the end of the day, the girls were ready for an early night. They had accomplished over half of the canning. Tomorrow, they would finish and all meet at Kayla's for supper. The husbands all came in at one time or another to give their wives a kiss goodnight before heading out to the offices or hotel. It was an early night for everyone.

The next morning began before the sun came up, the women determined to finish by supper. The men hoped to finish hauling straw and hay for the stables. The wood was all delivered and the chimneys taken care of, except Autumn's.

Jarod took the opportunity to do inventory, with the help of Mr. Wilson.

Hawk and Ben were going to the various family homes and making sure the meat sheds were all in order, the doors sturdy and locks working. By noon, the women were finished with the canning and had begun the dividing process. Each family had their wooden boxes to carry the jars home.

Just as they heard Samuel's wagon returning, the girls sat down with a collective sigh and cups of coffee. It was hard work, but in two days, the family was finished with the winter preparations. Everyone had wood, and the stable where the family kept all the horses and buggies and sleighs was full of oats and straw and hay. All that was left was to fill the meat lockers, and that always waited until it stayed frozen.

Samuel and Hawk had bought the old mill, cleaned it up and put their woodworking tools inside. They enjoyed making furniture and they had built up quite a business, keeping them busy most of the time.

Willow took Major, and after letting Hawk know, she and Missy went to her house to clean up for supper at Kayla's.

Everyone met at the restaurant at six sharp, for dinner. After they ordered their meal, the men began talking about all that was accomplished and all that needed to be done yet. The women were enjoying just sitting and relaxing after all their hard work, when, suddenly, Cheyenne, one of the Crooked Antler girls, came running up to Samuel.

"Mr. Samuel, Ada told me to hurry and get you boys. She said to tell you Harriet is missing. She didn't come down this afternoon, and when Ada went up, she was gone. She wants you to come right quick and talk to her." Cheyenne was worrying her dress, twisting it nervously in her hands, fear evident in her eyes.

She bent down, looking both ways to make sure no one was listening. "Mr. Samuel, you don't think those bad men got her, do you? We have been watching for them like you said. Mrs. Ada done showed us the picture you gave her."

The boys all stood up quickly.

"Excuse us, ladies, I will leave you all in Jarod and Brenden's capable hands. You girls all stay at Autumn's. Do not split up to go anywhere until we return. Do you all understand?" Lou questioned.

The girls agreed, and the men took off to the Crooked Antler, where a very worried Ada waited. As they entered the back door the girls use to go to their rooms, they could see Ada wringing her hands. She ran to them as soon as she saw them.

"Samuel, Harriet is gone. Her room is empty." Tears rolled down her old cheeks. "She was my youngest. No more than eighteen. I was so careful with her. I didn't let none of the rougher crowd have at her. I showed the girls your picture. They all knew not to go anywhere with either of those men. Please, Samuel, find her, please," the old woman begged, grabbing the lapel of his coat. "I may be an old whore, but I love these girls."

Lou shook his head. "I knew we would hear from them, sooner or later. Can you tell me anything at all? Who was the last gentleman to take her upstairs?"

Ada calmed down and turned to Cheyenne, asking, "Did you see her? It was your turn to watch out for her."

Cheyenne thought for a minute, then said, "That nice gentleman with a scar down his face. He always tips good. What was his name, um, Jerry, I think?"

Gabe calmly asked, "Could it have been Terry?"

"It could have been; it is always so noisy in there."

Lou and Samuel turned to Hawk. Samuel looked at his old friend as he turned to go to his horse with a grunt, "I can't guarantee I can find them. There are too many tracks leaving town. I can try, but I can't work miracles.

Ada ran to the old Indian. "All I can ask is that you try. Please help her."

Cheyenne ran to him, also. "He was with me last night. He asked me to go to a cattle shack outside of town. He never was rough with me. I don't understand? Terry has been coming here for two weeks now. Never any complaints."

Lou answered the girl, "He was using you to get information about our families, and when he was finished and had no more use for you, he became his normal, mean self."

Samuel looked at Hawk, Lou, and Gabe. "He wants us to find her. He is sending us a message. He knew Cheyenne would remember what he said, and he knows we will be coming for the girl. He has to be at the old Hart place, a couple hours out of town."

The men shook their heads. They were walking into a trap, but they knew every minute Harriet was with them, she would pay dearly.

Lou replied to Samuel, "She said he had a scar down his face. How did we miss that? Why were we not told? We need to go to the sheriff, so he can protect the girls while we are gone. It would be just like them to send us off on a wild goose chase, so they can snatch the girls."

Samuel agreed, "Let's get the sheriff and then head to the girls, to let them know what is going on so they are aware and can be extra vigilant."

As the sheriff and the men walked into Autumn and Jarod's home, they could see the dread in the girls' eyes. The worry that never seemed to leave anymore.

Samuel took Suzy on his lap before he looked at the rest of the family and said in a grim voice, "They snatched Harriet. Girls, look at me, Terry has a scar. Someone forgot to pass the information on to us. The brothers have set a trap, hoping we will fall into it."

Lou stood with Willow in his arms as he looked down at her and added, "I am hoping they are not luring us away to sneak back into town while we are gone. You girls need to stay right here with the sheriff and Jarod and Brenden." He then said to Brenden and Jarod, "I am counting on you to keep the women safe. Keep your rifles with you at all times. Samuel has rounded up several of your ranch hands to help guard the house. Do *not* leave the house for any reason. That also means if someone needs a doctor, Jarod. It could be a trap."

"I cannot help someone who needs a doctor, Lou? Perhaps you forgot I took an oath."

"Donald is at the clinic with Roger right now. There is no need for you to leave. We have explained everything to him. The deputy is stationed outside the clinic, and Ben and Starla are with them inside. They are safe. You stay here with the girls. We have to go, but we have a plan of our own. Every minute Harriet is with them will be pure pain for her."

He kissed Willow gently before bending down and looking into her frightened eyes. "Never fear, I have Hawk and Gabe and Samuel with me, along with some of Samuel's ranch hands. I will come home to you. I am counting on you to stay safe."

The men gave their wives kisses and hurried to their horses. They planned to lay a trap of their own. They had stopped at the hotel, where many of Samuel's men were staying for their days off. Gathering all the men they could, twenty hightailed it for the Hart place with them. Once they got within five miles or so, they split up. Ten went to the north with Hawk and Gabe, and the other ten went to the south with Samuel and Lou. Samuel knew they were only expecting between two to four men. They would not think of Samuel's ranchers. When they got within a half a mile of the cabin, they tied their horses. Samuel looked around carefully in the dark. Deeming it safe, the small group carefully and quietly walked the rest of the way, keeping their eyes open and their hands close to their guns.

Samuel's group was the first to arrive. Lou cupped his hands to give Samuel a boost, so he could look into the window. Samuel saw someone tied to a beam naked—long hair plastered to her back let him know it was a woman. He looked carefully around the rest of the room but saw no one. He didn't hear any sounds from inside. He gave Lou a nod and the other man lowered him to the ground.

Lou gave out the call of an owl to let the others know it was safe to come closer.

As some of the men gathered at the front door, the others stayed back in the woods surrounding the house.

Hawk stayed back, looking at the ground and the trees before too much of the evidence was disturbed. He carefully walked all around the area of the house and then began fanning further out, holding his torch high for light.

Samuel and Lou quietly opened the door of the hut, their guns drawn, taking the time to look around for any traps one more time. Lou looked to the naked woman hanging from the rafters. Rope was around her waist and arms, tying her arms to her sides. Blood dripped from her toes unto the floor. Lou turned away, bile threatening to choke him. He could see burns all over her body. Her breasts, bottom, and stomach had many shallow cuts and stab wounds—not enough to kill her. They were meant to cause pain. Blood ran down her legs from her pussy. A bullet hole to her head had finally killed her. She had not died easily. Samuel cut her down, and Lou wrapped her in a blanket to take back to Ada.

Lou turned to pick up a red rose on the table. A blood red silk rose, crushed, it's petals scattered across the table. A chill ran down his spine at the meaning. A rose for the Rose brothers. These men meant to have their wives to torture the same way they had Harriet. He looked at Gabe, who had also seen the rose and understood its meaning.

A fury filled Lou as he watched the men carry the woman out and lay her across the horse. Two men were chosen to ride with her to town and the sheriff before taking her to the undertaker. Samuel and the boys had the unpleasant job of telling Ada and the girls.

"We don't have a lot of time, Lou. We have to find out where they are holed up and take care of them," Gabe thought out load.

Lou agreed as Hawk continued looking for clues. It took time, but it was necessary.

"One horse has a cracked hoof; the other is a bigger horse. That's the one that carried the girl. I found some hair on this branch. It's black, which tells me one of the horses is black. The hoof prints lead to the mountains. There are many caves in those mountains. They did make a fire and eat before they left, maybe an hour or two ago. I also found a bloody knife. Not a typical knife; this one has a carved handle. It is an expensive one, not one an escaped prisoner could afford. They have money, either taken from people they have killed or stolen. I will come back with Samuel, tomorrow, and together, we will look around some more. I would like Brenden and his men to take Little Bird and Suzy home in the morning, where they can be guarded better."

"You can do what you want with your wives, but I want Suzy home," Samuel stated with conviction, confirming how the older men felt. "There are plenty of men to help guard the women in town. I will leave some of my hands in town to help out," Samuel finished.

Lou and Gabe agreed. It would be better to have the girls stay in town. They could stay with family and be safe while Lou and Gabe, along with Samuel and Hawk, went on the hunt.

All four of the men went to the Crooked Antler before they went home. Ada was a crying mess and the rest of the girls were all scared to death, standing huddled together to comfort one another. They had heard that Harriet was found.

"Ada, why don't you shut down your part of the saloon for a few days? Give the girls a rest and give us some time to find these men and bring them to justice. There are two of them. I am not sure that they aren't your customers."

Ada nodded her head. "I will spread the word to the other saloons in town and let them know one of them has a scar. I'll make sure they know what happened to poor Harriet."

Samuel took Ada in his arms, rocking her as she began to sob again. Finally, when she had calmed down again, he said softly, "The men and I took up a collection to pay for the girl's funeral." He handed her a wad of bills.

"Thank you, Samuel. You and yours are good people. I will do all I can to help you catch these men."

Samuel grunted as he let her go and turned to the others, saying, "Let's get back to the women and let them know what is going on. We will take Brenden and Spring and the wives to the hotel. I will have some of my men guarding it tonight. We will leave in the morning as soon as I can load everything up. We'll come back as soon as we see to the safety of our families."

"We'll leave some of Brenden's men to guard the block you and Jarod live on. They can stay until we send replacements back to relieve them. We need to organize our hired hands, so they can guard the ranch and help out in town. We can't spread them too thin," Hawk finished.

As the men returned home, they finished making their plans.

After explaining everything to the women, they took their families either home or to the hotel. Wynter and Summer stayed with Jarod and Autumn.

Lou carried Willow home in his arms, her head on his shoulders and Major following behind. The dog seemed to know Lou was rattled. Lou set Willow down and unlocked the door, carefully looking into every room before he came back and retrieved her. He walked over to the fireplace and neatly stacked some wood. He seemed to need time to think before he turned to her.

She could see Lou was bothered greatly by what had happened. His eyes looked haunted and worried. She walked over to him as he finished lighting the fire. "It is getting cold at night; winter can't be far behind."

Lou looked at her and just grunted. His mind was far away in thought.

Willow decided she would take his mind off his worries for a while. She heated water and filled the tub while Lou sat at the table with a cup of fresh coffee. When his bath was ready, she called him over and helped him undress. He sank slowly into the steaming water, his muscles relaxing as he sat back.

"Mmm, this feels so good," he moaned as the heated water continued to relax him.

She returned with the soap and shampoo. Running plenty of water over his head, she began washing his dark hair, massaging his scalp before she rinsed his hair. She took up the soap and lathered her hands before she began washing his back, rubbing the tight muscles as she ran her hands over his tanned skin. She came to his front side and began lathering. A naughty twinkle could be seen clearly in her eyes as Lou looked up at her while she slowly ran her hands down his shoulders to his chest and stomach. A smile crossed his face as he watched her move to his now rock-hard cock.

Even after all this time married to him, she was still learning how to please him. Her innocence had always amazed him. He took his time with her, never rushing her to do things she wasn't ready for. He let her learn at her own pace.

Her hands wrapped around his cock, her fingers not touching—he was as big down there as he was everywhere else. Her hands went from the bottom of his cock to the top, pulling the skin, squeezing, until Lou threw his head back and moaned.

She smiled before she stopped to rinse him, then stood and held out a large, thick towel. As he stepped out, she wrapped it around his waist and took his hand to lead him to the chair in front of the fireplace. The fire was, by this time, dancing merrily, keeping the bedroom toasty warm. She sat him down and began drying his hair with another towel. Gathering the brush, she quickly put his hair in order. It was longer than fashionable but not overly long, and he liked to keep it neat. She came to the front of him and lifted the towel from his lap. Slowly, ever so slowly, she sank to her knees in front of him and took his cock into her hand to guide it to her mouth. She looked up at him with a smile before she lowered her mouth onto him and began to gently suck. Her hands went to his balls, and she gently massaged them as her head bobbed up and down in a slow rhythm that had him gripping the edge of his seat, his head back and a moan escaping his lips. She began sucking harder and faster. Not able to take him all, she did the best she could. His moans became louder. When his balls tightened, he moaned her name, "Willow, stop, if you don't want to go all the way. I am about to explode."

Willow stopped for just a second, uncertain whether to continue. She had never come this far before. It was a first time for her. She closed her eyes and continued with vigor as Lou put his hands into her hair. She continued until she felt his muscles tighten, his hands gripping her head, holding it onto his cock as streams of his essence found its way down her throat. She continued until he was finished. Licking her lips, she looked up at him.

He had a smile on his face as he looked at her with pride. He stood and led her to the bed. "I am so proud of you, little one. You did very good for your first time." He turned her to unbutton her lovely dress, letting it pool at her feet as he helped her step out of it. Pulling down the straps to her slip, he began kissing her shoulders and neck. As he lowered the straps, he kissed further down, until the slip fell to the floor and it joined the dress. He laid her onto the bed and began gently sucking her breasts, first one and then the other, plucking at the neglected one.

Willow began moaning, twisting this way and that as the pleasure built. He moved down further, his tongue leaving a trail of fire down her stomach. She opened her legs as he got closer to her pleasure center and began sucking gently on her little nub. Willow squealed in delight, lifting her bottom off the bed. Her nub became engorged and her juices flowed as she moaned his name. She began begging, "Please, Lou, please go in. I need you, please."

Lou crawled between her legs, positioning himself at her entrance before he impaled her. He took her with an urgency, like he might not have her tomorrow, pounding into her trying to erase the picture of Harriet hanging in the rafters. The look of pure terror in the girl's eyes was imprinted on his mind. Willow opened her legs wider, allowing him more access. She knew he needed it rough tonight. She knew her husband had demons, and she knew how to help him. He put her legs on his massive shoulders, bringing her sex closer, opening her more to him. He continued until he felt his balls tighten and felt her pussy spasm with the coming explosion. He roared his release just as she screamed his name, and they both came apart. He continued pumping until the very last drop of his essence had entered her. He rolled off her as he put his arm over his eyes, willing his heart to slow and his breathing to become normal again. Once he knew Willow had calmed down some, he went to the washbowl and came back to the bed, cleaning them both. He pulled Willow into his arms. His little Willow. The woman he would die for. His reason for living. He pulled the blankets over them, and in the security of his arms, she fell asleep. It took Lou much longer.

She woke to Lou thrashing and twisting, moaning in his sleep. He had these nightmares occasionally, but they had become rare the last few months. She tried to wake him, but he was deep into the dream.

"Lou, sweetheart, wake up." She shook him but to no avail.

He began to shout, "Leave her alone, or I will kill you."

With his eyes wide open in terror, he sat straight up, looking wildly for Willow. His eyes adjusted enough to find her huddled in the bed with the blankets up to her chin. He had frightened her. He reached out to her and pulled her into his embrace. "Thank God. Thank God, Willow. You are safe," he whispered over and over as he rocked her. She put her little hand on his chest.

"Shh, Lou, I am fine."

Lou held her close, so she could not see the tears streaming down his cheeks as he rocked her.

THE NEXT MORNING, Lou woke to the smell of breakfast. As he walked into the kitchen, Willow looked at her strong, handsome husband. He didn't bother putting on his shirt as he walked to the door to let Major out. The dark hair on his chest was the sexiest; she always longed to run her hands over the muscles of his chest and shoulders.

Willow poured his coffee and put his plate down before him as she waited for him to pull out her chair. They ate in silence until she brought up the dream.

Lou looked at her sadly before he spoke. "It was nothing. Another nightmare, like the rest. Don't fret on it."

Willow grinned. "If I lied that big, I would get a spanking."

Lou simply smiled at her.

"Maybe we made a baby last night, Lou."

She saw him stiffen before he turned and looked at her. There was no humor in his eyes. Just dead serious intent as he said, "I will wait at the office for Samuel and Hawk after I walk you to the clinic. Willow, I need you to stay with Autumn until I return. It may take a couple of days, but I mean to find these men."

"That's fine, Lou. Is Missy still being guarded by the deputy and some of Samuel's ranch hands?" She could feel him pulling away from her and it hurt.

"Yes, and if she wants to visit, she needs to visit you at Autumn's. I don't want you to stick your cute little nose out of the house after work. Is that understood?"

Willow nodded. "Yes, sir."

Willow walked to the back door to let Major in. A scream had Lou running.

In the snow, near the bedroom window, Major stood whining and pawing at the snow. Willow pointed to footprints.

A rage took hold of Lou that he had trouble controlling. "Get in the house!" he shouted to her. He snapped his fingers at Major, who followed her in. The footprints led to their bedroom window—a man's large boots with spurs. When Lou thought of what they had done last night, he began to shake. He ran back into the house, locking the doors, checking all the windows. He put on his shirt and coat. Turning to Willow, he shouted at her to get ready to go to Autumn's.

"Take a couple days' worth of clothes," he commanded in a loud voice.

Willow quickly did as he instructed, not being used to Lou talking to her like this. She gathered her coat quickly, and they walked to Autumn's. Autumn was talking to Storm as they entered, and Lou went to find Jarod in his back office.

When he came out, he could hear Autumn telling Storm, "That is why you two should also stay here. We have plenty of room, and it is safer here. Also," she looked at Storm, "Wynter is so big now, I think she needs to stay closer to the clinic. She could go into labor any time, and what if you are at the courthouse and she is outside of town?"

Storm agreed, but Wynter wanted to argue, "I don't want to be a bother, Mom."

Autumn sighed, "Wynter, you are no bother, and I would like it if you would think of the worrying I do."

Jarod spoke up next, "You two will stay here. That is the end of the discussion. Storm, tonight, you can go and get your things. Use the big spare room, where you will have some privacy, and Willow can use the smaller spare room. When we built this house, I was hoping to fill it with children. It didn't work out that way." He walked to Autumn and held her. "But we have plenty of room for grown children. It will be closer for Storm, and you will be closer to the clinic. Now that all of that is settled, Willow, let's go to the clinic. Come on, Major."

Lou walked quickly to the office, and after he explained what had happened to Gabe and Ben, he took a walk out back. Sure enough, there were footsteps going up to the back fence where the younger dogs were trained. They walked all around the house.

"The same ones as at my house, boots, with spurs."

"I wonder what they were looking for? Ben hasn't let the dogs out yet this morning. Let's look around." Sure, enough, in the dog's dish was fresh meat. Gabe gave it a smell. "The meat has got something bad in it. Them son of a bitches tried to poison Ben's pups."

The men took the dish into the office to show Ben.

"Best not let the dogs out until you check the area, Ben," Missy spoke up from the stove. "I will keep Starla here with me."

Just then, Samuel and Hawk came striding in. When they explained everything to them, Samuel shook his head. "They must have back tracked back to town last night. Beats me where they are hiding out."

Lou said, "I had the paper print off more copies of the pictures and wrote on the bottom that there was a scar on one of them. We need to see if we can get a more up to date picture to pass around, but until then, let's split up and hand one out to everyone in town and nearby. I will post one in the clinic. Gabe, can you see to the bank and library and museum? Samuel and Hawk, can you give the saloons in town another? Make sure they know the pictures are not up to date. I will go to the telegraph and post office and the sheriff's again. I need to telegraph the governor and try to get a newer picture or an idea what happened. I also have to let him know about Harriet. Ben, please stay here with Missy until the deputy comes to take her to the school."

Hawk added, although it was not necessary, "Don't be afraid to ask a lot of questions. The more we find out, the faster we can find them. They have to be hiding somewhere close."

Everyone had their jobs and began immediately. By the time it grew dark, the air had become colder and the wind had changed.

Hawk looked up at the sky. "It's going to snow tonight. What do you think, Samuel, should we spend the night at the hotel?"

Samuel agreed, "We can get an early start in the morning." Turning to Lou, he added, "How about breakfast at your house, in the morning?"

"I am sure Willow would love it. It's her weekend off. We can leave from there. Missy, would you like to visit Willow at Autumn's, tomorrow?"

Missy happily nodded her head. "Oh, yes, please, Gabe. Autumn and I have a bunch of crocheting to do for the church. I, um, volunteered this year. They go to the poor, and Willow promised to help me."

Lou laughed as he told Gabe, "You know those old biddies kept bothering Willow to volunteer until I finally put my foot down. The women of the church go around gossiping about everyone instead of getting others to help out, and Willow was getting all the work. Between that and the clinic, she was getting worn out. Just a warning to keep an eye out." Lou slapped Gabe on the back.

Gabe replied with a grin, "Thanks for the warning."

When Lou arrived at the clinic, Jarod told him that Neil, one of

Brenden's men, had volunteered to walk Willow and Major home, and he would wait with her until Lou returned before he left.

Lou whistled as he left the clinic. As soon as he walked into the house, he could smell a delicious supper waiting for him—steaks and baked potato and kohlrabi, all piping hot and just coming off the stove. Neil was helping Willow put everything on the table. He turned to look at Lou as he entered. He was just a boy of about twenty-two years, but Brenden only had the best hired help. Lou knew this man could be trusted.

"Willow said if I took her home and stayed with her, she would feed me."

The boy clearly had a bad case of hero worship. Lou smiled to himself. He had felt that same way when Samuel had taken him under his wing. It was time to pass it on to the younger men.

"Where are your folks, boy?"

"Ma lives in town, but my pa died a few years back of smallpox. I needed to help Ma out; that's why I hired on with Samuel. Been working for him for a couple of years now," he said with pride.

"He has taught me a lot in those years. This last few months, I have started working with Brenden and his family."

Lou nodded. "Proud to know ya, kid."

"I will have a hot meal every night for both of you, if he will continue to walk me home after work and stay, so I can get some work done at the house."

Lou smiled at the young man. Good home cooking was hard to come by for a ranch hand. "I will pay you if you become her personal guard. I'll talk to Brenden. You pick her up and stay with her until I get home and I will make it worth it, along with a home cooked meal every night. Mind you, I am trusting you to stick to her like glue and to protect her, no matter what."

Neil nodded happily. "I would do anything for you men, Lou. Gosh, you are like a hero in these parts."

"I am no hero, boy; neither is any of the rest of us. We are just men, flesh and blood men. Thanks for the compliment, though. Is it a deal, then?"

"Deal! I promise I won't let anything happen to her, sir. Not when I can get meals like this."

The thought of someone with Willow while she did what made her happy made Lou very content. He smiled as the young man moaned at the first bite of Willow's famous biscuits.

"Hawk says snow tonight. I will go and talk to Samuel, so he can get word to Brenden. If you would care to stay during the nights in the spare room on the other side of the kitchen, we can both have some privacy and Willow doesn't need to stay at Autumn's during the evenings anymore. She can come home with you and do what she feels she needs to do."

"That is fine by me. Beats staying with a bunch of smelly men at the hotel."

Willow laughed. "You have your own water closet." She turned to Lou. "I had him light the fire in the laundry room, so we can have some hot water. If I am to stay home, we can leave it lit and have hot water whenever we want."

While they sat and sipped some good hot coffee, Lou explained to Neil exactly what he wanted. Neil agreed and understood everything. The men stood, patting their stomachs before they helped Willow clean the table.

"I will go and get my things from the hotel when you return from talking to Samuel. May I take Major for a walk with me, as long as you are home?"

Willow said to Neil, "I am sure he would love the exercise, and I will be perfectly safe with Lou. You are free to do whatever you want while I am at the clinic."

As Willow finished the dishes, Neil let Major out to do his business. This would work out nicely, Willow thought.

As Neil left to get his things, Lou and Willow stood in the doorway and watched the first snowflakes fall—fat, fluffy snowflakes that looked like diamonds in the streetlight. Lou pulled her close to keep her warm as they stood and watched as they came down harder. After a few more minutes, he pulled her into the house and put another couple logs onto the fire. He then went into the back bedroom and started the fire for Neil and went into their room to stir the fire to life again in there.

Willow smiled as her husband puttered around the house. When Neil returned, the couple turned into their room with Major. The house was soon quiet.

THE BABIES

The next couple of weeks went by quickly, and everything seemed normal again. Wynter was getting bigger by the day, and it was getting harder for her to get around. Jarod had finally insisted she either sit and take it easy more or stay in bed. She chose to sit.

On some of her days off, Missy and Willow spent them with Jarod's family. Autumn and the girls were crocheting blankets for the baby and for the church. Missy was not good at crocheting, so Willow worked on them more. This suited Missy just fine, never one to miss an opportunity to pass work on to Willow. She planned to tell the church she did them and wouldn't mention Willow at all.

Willow understood the game and didn't mind that Missy took credit for the work. Missy was her friend.

On one quiet night, there came a pounding on the door. Storm came in a wild look in his eyes. "Jarod had to leave to deliver a baby, but suddenly, Wynter is in terrible pain. Autumn said to come and get you. Hurry, Willow, she is hurting bad. I think the baby is coming."

Willow hurried down the street just a few houses while Lou

followed. Inside, Wynter was on the bed moaning and holding her stomach.

"Oh, Willow, it hurts. It hurts so bad. Help me please."

Willow shooed everyone out and lifted the blankets off the lower part of Wynter's body. She lifted her gown. While she examined her, she hummed. This was her calling; she had birthed many babies on her own while Jarod was off and gone. Her humming calmed Wynter some. When Willow finished, she called out for a glass of cold water.

"Wynter, you are barely dilated. If you are in labor, it is in the very early stages. I think this is false labor."

Wynter moaned, "It can't be false, Willow, it hurts. Please don't tell me this is the beginning and not the end."

"I have some willow bark tea for you to drink; it will calm you and help you to sleep. I will stay until your pa comes home.

Storm came in with the water as Willow explained to him what she thought. Autumn brought in the tea and Willow stayed to make sure she drank every drop. It wasn't long before Wynter was curled up in the blankets, sleeping peacefully.

Willow explained to Storm, "She is just starting to dilate. She will have the baby in the next few days. That is my prediction, but I would have Jarod check her over when he comes home.

Willow and Lou sat with Storm and Autumn while they waited for Jarod to return. Autumn made some more willow bark tea for Wynter in case she woke up, and Storm paced back and forth. Willow answered all of his questions about labor and the birth. Willow had a secret that only Jarod and she knew, but she was sworn to secrecy by Jarod. He was not positive and didn't want to give any false hope.

Finally, a tired Jarod came home late that night and Willow explained what she had found before she and Lou returned home. Once they were home and in their own bed, very quickly, Willow fell asleep in Lou's arms.

The routine at the clinic stayed basically the same. Roger was staying the night at the clinic in the spare room, so he didn't have to travel outside of town to his home. He took Major for a walk every lunch hour to the graveyard and back. Major loved the exercise, and Willow had a suspicion Major loved Roger, too. Roger was walking much better because of his almost daily treks. It eased Jarod's mind to have someone at the clinic at night as they had many dangerous drugs locked in the cabinets. Roger always helped clean up every night, and, in return, Jarod or Storm always took him a plate of Autumn's delicious suppers, making sure the old man had a good hot meal. He usually came in the morning for breakfast with Jarod, also. Jarod was more than happy with the arrangement, and Willow loved the old man dearly.

Everything had been quiet until, one afternoon, the Wyatt boys and their friends came into town. They usually came after roundup in the spring or in the fall, but this day, they came with their sister to do some early shopping. As usual, the boys and their hired hands got drunk and raised a fuss. The sheriff always called on Lou and Gabe to help round them up and put them in jail until their pa could come and get them. But, this time, they had Julie with them. So, when the boys rounded them up and put them in jail, Lou had to ride out to their pa's ranch with her and let old Caleb know he was needed in town again.

Neil stayed with Willow until Lou returned, grumbling about the ole man who didn't take a stick to his boys long ago.

"Those boys and the hands they have for friends are going to get themselves in deep trouble, one of these days, and that ole man will have no one to blame but himself. I know their ma died when they were young, but that ole man didn't do them boys any favors by letting them run wild. Ada has her girls working again, and they get too rough with them. Ada damn near shot Matthew. Luckily, we got there in time to save his worthless hide. I told Caleb his boys are not welcome at the Crooked Antler anymore."

Willow just laughed. "Calm down, Lou, supper is ready."

As Lou finished his supper and helped Willow clean up, Neil took Major for a short walk.

A pounding on the door startled Willow out of her thoughts. She had a secret she wanted to share with Lou. She wanted to wait a couple more weeks until she was sure, but it took all she had not to spill the beans.

Storm came running in. "Jarod says to tell you it is for real, this time. He needs you at the clinic." He looked around wildly until he saw Lou. "Please let everyone else know that Wynter is having our baby." He grabbed Willow and her coat, dragging her out the door.

Lou laughed as he waited for Neil to return. As soon as he could, he saddled his big black stallion and galloped off to Mark and Summer's home to give them the good news. He then asked Tom to ride to the hotel and get Samuel. They had brought the ladies back with them when Willow told them the baby would come any time. Once he was sure the family all knew, he headed to the clinic. He knew the routine by this time. The family would wait in the waiting room for word. Samuel and the men would keep Storm calmed down with some of Samuel's best whiskey.

As he entered, he saw Storm pacing back and forth, stopping every time he heard Wynter moan. Shaking his head, he would continue pacing.

Samuel and Hawk and Suzy and Little Bird came behind Lou, and following in the rear was Gabe and Missy. Samuel evaluated the situation as soon as he entered. He took Storm by the arm and led him and the others outside. Once outside, he pulled out the bottle and passed it to Storm first. Storm shook his head, but Samuel insisted. He took a small sip, but when he heard Wynter moan even louder, he took another good drink before passing it to Lou.

Inside, Roger brought out a tray of tea. He passed the cups to all the ladies who were waiting patiently. Taking the tray back with him, he soon came out with a tray of cookies that Autumn had made that very day. In fact, they were still warm.

Inside the birthing room, Wynter struggled to keep the moaning to a minimum. She knew it was tearing Storm up to hear her in pain. She held onto the leather straps on the birthing table, gritting her teeth as another scream wanted to escape. She begged Jarod and Willow, "Please get it out of me. Please." Tears rolled down her cheeks. "Papa, please help me."

Jarod was working as fast as nature allowed. Something was wrong, and his hands were too big to do the job. He turned to Willow. "Please see if one of them is twisted or caught."

Willow put her small hands inside and felt that the baby was breach and had its little leg caught on the pelvic bone. She gently twisted and pulled until the tiny foot came free. It was not long before the *first* baby appeared. Willow quickly wrapped him in a towel and took him to the warm water that was waiting to clean the newest baby of the family. She then put him in the crib, wrapped in a warm blanket. She returned just in time to see the second one being born. She again took the tiny little boy, cleaned and wrapped him, putting him next to his brother. Jarod was preparing the ether and Willow was preparing the sutures, when Wynter began to moan again. Expecting her to expel the afterbirth, Willow retrieved the bowl, only to see a little head.

"Oh my, Jarod, another."

Jarod looked over, confused, as Willow caught another baby, a little girl. She giggled. "Storm never did anything in half measures." She took the tiny girl, cleaned her and wrapped her, putting her with her two brothers.

Wynter was asleep as soon as Jarod gave her a tiny bit of ether and Willow stitched her up.

Outside in the waiting room, all the family waited patiently, except Storm. As he heard the last scream, it took all Samuel and Lou had to hold him from barging into the birthing room. They finally got him calmed down.

Autumn shook her finger in his face. "You have been through

this enough to know we must wait until mother and baby are prepared for company."

"But, Mother Autumn, I thought I heard two distinct cries. Could there be two?"

Autumn smiled a knowing smile. "Could be, son, it just could be. We will have to wait until we are called."

Just as Willow came out and crooked her finger at Storm, Wynter was waking up. Jarod had put the little girl to her mother's breast. Storm walked over to her, his eyes full of wonder and pride. "A little girl, Momma. I am so proud of you."

Wynter just smiled as Jarod cleared his throat and led Storm to the crib where the two boys were sucking on their little fists. They were patiently waiting their turn at the tit, seeming to know their little sister needed it more.

Storm looked up in shock.

Jarod just shook his head. "Yep, three of them."

Jarod led him to the chair next to the bed, where he sat down and looked back and forth from the little girl to the crib.

"My darling, three? How did we accomplish that?"

Wynter replied wearily, smiling, "I don't know, but aren't we the luckiest parents in the whole world? Two boys and a girl to love."

One of the boys was beginning to cry, so Willow put a pillow on Wynter's other side and gave the baby the other tit.

As soon as the babies had eaten, Jarod invited the rest of the family to come in, deciding it was best to let them all in as usual and then shoo them all out, so Wynter could get some much-needed sleep.

Everyone was so surprised at the news of triplets. Autumn knew about the possibility of twins, but she wasn't prepared for a third baby. They all cooed and awed as the men stood back to let the ladies in first. Samuel learned early on, it wasn't worth his life to butt-in in front of one of the women before they had their fill.

∽

The clinic was busy the next couple of weeks, when colds and the flu started making the rounds. The two grandmothers helped Wynter with the babies, and Storm found a wet nurse to help with the feeding, but Wynter insisted on using her as little as possible. She wanted that bond with the children.

Neil took every other weekend off to go home to his ma and they coordinated it with Willow's weekends off. Willow spent much of her time with Autumn, crocheting to help Missy fill her quota to the church. Everyone was kept busy with the babies. Summer made many new nightgowns and Lori donated booties to the cause, while Spring and Anna Mae cut and sewed soft nappies.

THE DREAM AND A KILLER

Lou came home later and later, the frustration and worry showing on his face. He'd had two more nightmares since the first one, and Willow was at her wits' end as to how to help him. He had come home well after supper, this night, to pick up Willow, and while they walked quietly home, Willow peeked up at her husband. His face was pinched, his forehead wrinkled in worry. His eyes were tired from the lack of sleep the nightmares were robbing from him. He looked angry and exhausted. Willow held his arms, hoping to offer him comfort.

He reached over, patting it. His face softened as he looked down at her. When they reached the house, Lou left her outside with Major and, as usual, went inside to look around and make sure no one had gotten in. Willow heard a roar.

"God damn it!" he yelled.

Willow jumped at his shouted words. He normally didn't swear around her. Major stayed with Willow, on the alert, crowding her side. Lou came out for her. The look on his face scared her. She had never seen him so angry. On the table was a red rose. Someone had gotten into their home. Lou took her by the arm and led her back to Autumn and Jarod's home. He explained everything to Jarod before he turned to leave. Even though he was dog tired, he went back to the house and began checking for footprints and evidence. He went to the office and enlisted Gabe's help, and they followed the footsteps around the house, then lost them in the road when they became mixed with other tracks. They finally came up with the way someone had entered the house. Gabe spotted the open window near the laundry tub in the basement. The water used to do laundry and heat water for the bath was stored in a large tub underground. There was a door into the large butter room off the end of the house where Lou could go down and add more wood to keep the water hot. The latch was broken, the lock on the floor.

Gabe and Lou went down to look around and found nothing else amiss. The water from the run off of the hills just past the back yard was still blocked off, waiting to dump into the large vat. The fire was out, as usual, only to be used when needed to do laundry or for a hot bath. Both men worked to fix the door, putting a larger latch and lock on it. Lou also put a bar across it, so no one could enter again unless they were invited.

"I hate being a prisoner in my own home, damn it."

"We have bolted the door between the apartments and the office, too, Lou. I will also put a bar on it. They seem to be targeting you and yours, first." Gabe looked seriously into Lou's eyes. He was worried about his friend. They all were aware he wasn't sleeping.

"What is up with you, Lou? You have been dog assed tired the last few weeks, not yourself. Your temper is short, and you look like you are ready to explode."

Lou told him about the nightmares, and Gabe shook his head. "I thought you were pretty much done with those."

"I see Willow lying in the street. I can't tell who it is, but this man looks like a gun fighter. His gun is tied down and his hat keeps me from seeing his face." Lou gulped before he could continue. "Willow is lying in a pool of blood."

Gabe looked at his friend for a few minutes before he replied with, "Your last dream came true, if I remember right."

Lou nodded. "They do, most of the time. I can avoid what happens if I take precautions, sometimes, but Willow doesn't want to leave. I suggested Janie's in Boston. Jarod said he would telegraph his sister, but you know how that turned out. Both girls refused. I don't want to force her."

Gabe scratched his head. "I won't send Missy. I can protect her better here, with her family all around."

Lou answered, "I know, but you are not the one having the nightmares. No one broke into your home. It's not Missy I see in the street."

"Leave Willow at Jarod's, tonight. She is probably sleeping by now, anyway. Stay here and try to get some rest. Don't come in until you have had some sleep. I'll talk to Samuel about this, in the morning. I can't use you like this. Stay home with Willow, tomorrow." Gabe left his friend to fight his demons. He needed to be alone for a while until he could get control of himself.

Lou knew Gabe was right. He was not helping while he was like this. He wandered over to the cupboard and got down the bottle of whiskey, filling his glass to the top, before he went to add wood to the fire. When he was finished, he sat at the table and, in one gulp, emptied the glass. He would sleep tonight.

The next morning, he woke with a sore head, but he had slept like a rock. Sleep was what he needed the most. He went to retrieve his wife. He wanted to spend the day with her.

Willow gladly went home with him. She spent most of the day cooking and cleaning.

Lou took her to Missy's home later, to deliver some of the crocheting, and while they were there, he talked with Gabe, slapping him on the back.

"I got good and drunk and slept like a baby. What did Samuel say?"

I told Samuel you were having dreams again. He asked me what about, and I told him. He was really surprised you didn't come to him, Lou. Kind of disappointed."

Lou shook his head. "I thought I could get a hold of it, but they kept coming more and more often. I should have said something, I know, but damn it, a man has to protect his own family."

Just then, Samuel walked in with Hawk, frustration written all over their faces.

"They have to be hiding somewhere near or in town, but I will be damned if I can tell where."

Lou looked at Samuel. This was the man whom he had thought of as a father. He felt ashamed that he had let his pride get in the way of asking this great man for help.

"Samuel, I owe you men an apology. I am sorry for not confiding in you about something this important."

Samuel just grunted before looking Lou right in the eye. "I understand it was personal, boy. But sometimes, you have to talk to family. Let's move on."

Willow and Missy came skipping down the stairs, smiling at the men. Major followed behind with a bone in his mouth, compliments of Ben.

"Willow and I think we should all go out to Kayla's for supper and forget about all this ruckus for the night."

Samuel smiled at the mischievous girl. "You both think that, do you?"

Willow nodded happily. "Yep, we do. We need a night without thinking about these ghost men."

Hawk agreed, "We all could give it a rest for one night. I think it is a good idea."

The seven of them walked over to Kayla's. The wind had picked up again, giving the night a chill. The good food and warm company was just what the doctor ordered. They talked about everything but Terry and Willard. Ben was explaining where he was with the pups' training, and Hawk talked about going hunting sometime in the next week. He invited all the men to join in for one day of hunting for meat and the skins he would take back to Little Bird. They all agreed on a day to hunt. The girls decided to get together at Autumn's and do some crocheting for the babies that day.

"I will see if it is all right with Autumn and let you know," Willow told Missy.

Willow could see the men relaxing as they sat back and drank their coffee. For the first time in a long while, the worry lines on Lou's face seemed to be relaxing. He had a smile on his face as they discussed the hunting trip.

They spotted Autumn and Jarod having dinner. Everyone needed some time to relax, it seemed.

Suddenly, Cheyenne ran up to Samuel, her eyes wide with fright. "Miss Ada told me to get you quick. She says to tell you that man with a scar has Celia in her room. She said to hurry."

All the men jumped up. Lou and Gabe took the girls apologetically to Jarod and Autumn's table quickly, explaining while Hawk and Samuel paid the bill.

The four men and Cheyenne took off for the stable. Ben had run back and had begun saddling the horses. He had corralled Neil on the way. All four horses were saddled by the time the men entered. Hoisting Cheyenne up behind Samuel, they took off at a gallop. Ada was waiting nervously when they arrived, minutes later.

"Celia gave the signal when Terry approached her, just like I taught them. He is in the last room on the right with her now. Please hurry."

A blood-curdling scream came from upstairs.

Samuel took the steps two at time, with the others close behind. Another scream, and Samuel had his gun drawn and kicked open the door.

Terry stood over the bed with a knife in his hand, raised to strike. Celia was huddled in the corner, naked, her eyes wide with fright, her mouth open to let out another scream.

Terry turned to Samuel with a wicked smile on his face before he turned back to the frightened girl. He lunged for her just as

Samuel fired. The bullet entered his head, only to exit right between the eyes. Celia screamed again, right before she fainted dead away.

Hawk ran up to Terry, quickly looking through his pockets for any clue as to where they were staying. All he came up with was about a hundred dollars in bills. He handed them to Ada. "She earned them tonight."

He pulled the dead man over his shoulders before he turned to exit the room. "I will take him to the undertaker."

Samuel replied, "The cheapest box, and tell him to bury him on the hill in a pauper's grave. I will have the sheriff send the reward money to the orphanage."

Everyone agreed with the arrangements. Lou lifted Celia and took her to the next room while Gabe took the bloody sheets and threw them in the fire. They all left together.

Samuel spoke first. "Well, that is one of them. Now, to find the other."

Lou nodded as he added his thoughts, "It's only going to piss Willard off. He will want some terrible revenge for this. We all have to keep an extra eye out for everyone in the family."

Everyone agreed about that, also.

Gabe got his two cents in. "Let's hope he is so mad, he makes a stupid mistake."

The men went to Autumn and Jarod's to retrieve their wives. They had done a good night's work tonight. They had rid themselves and the town of a madman. But, somehow, the men were more afraid now than ever before.

Two mornings later, they discovered what Willard's revenge was.

Willow had just finished cleaning the kitchen after breakfast. Lou had left a few minutes earlier, leaving Neil with her. Suddenly, she heard the key in the door. The door flew open, and filling the entire doorway was Lou, looking wildly until his gaze found

Willow. She could see the relief flood his face before sorrow filled it again.

He whispered, "Thank God, Willow." He nodded for Neil to leave as he unbuckled his gun belt and laid it on the table next to the rocker.

Willow became worried. Something was terribly wrong. "Lou, what's wrong? You are scaring me."

Lou took his wife by the hand and led her to the rocker. He hated to hurt her, but she had to know. If he didn't tell her, she would learn of it seconds after leaving for work. He didn't want her to see what had happened to her friend. He pulled her onto his lap and pulled her head onto his chest over his heart. "Willow, Willard killed Roger last night."

Willow struggled to rise up, but Lou would not allow her to get up. He kissed her gently, looking into her eyes as the tears filled them. He continued rocking her as first one tear rolled down her cheek and then another, until there was a steady stream and, finally, a sob broke out. He held her tight, telling her all he knew.

"Jarod went to see why he had not come to breakfast. He found him on the floor, the damn rose next to him. I have not been there yet. I came right here as soon as I got word. Gabe is at the clinic now, going through all the evidence, and Hawk and Samuel are on their way from the hotel." He knew the sooner he got on the trail, the better the chance of capturing this killer, but, right now, his first priority was to Willow.

Jarod entered their house, grief written on his face. His hands were shaking as he did all he could to keep calm and to keep the tears from falling. "Samuel is taking the body to the undertaker's." He looked at Willow, sitting on Lou's lap.

"I am sorry, Willow. I know he meant a lot to you. He meant a lot to me, too." His voice hitched. "We have to catch this monster." He then addressed Lou, "Please bring Willow to my house when she is ready. The other men are waiting for you. Gabe has news you should know. We will watch over her."

Lou let Willow stand, wiping the tears from her eyes, "Go, Lou, and catch this man and make him pay."

Jarod looked at Willow. "I will ask the minister to have services, tomorrow. They will not bury him until spring, but we can have our services. Can you send the sheriff to my home to watch over our families until I do what needs to be done, Lou?"

Lou nodded before he strapped on his holster again. "I'll walk you home and then send over the sheriff. I am sure he is at the clinic by now."

When Willow arrived, the girls were all in an embrace, crying and trying to comfort one another.

In a shaky voice, Jarod gave the girls their orders, "Willow and the rest of you girls, stay here. You do not need to see this. There is no doubt who did this. He was cut up bad."

As the sheriff arrived, Jarod went to speak to the minister and then returned to the clinic.

Samuel, Hawk, Gabe and Lou cleaned up the mess and took the old man to the undertaker's, so no one else need see what a mad man can do to a human body.

Gabe had found a note under the rose with three words on it. "Willow is next."

He handed it to Lou as soon as he entered. Every man watched Lou's expression turn to pure rage before it turned to terror. He ran to Jarod's to find his Willow in the embrace of Suzy and Little Bird. The rest of the men followed.

Lou went to Willow, gathering her in his arms and holding her like he was afraid of losing her. He looked over to Jarod and ever so slightly nodded his head. Jarod knew what Lou needed him to do. The men had all discussed it, but he was still conflicted. "Are you sure, Lou?"

Lou stared at the man for a moment before he answered with total conviction, "I am sure." He continued to rock his wife, carrying her to the rocker and putting her on his lap. He held her tightly. He had made a decision that might very well cost him his little wife, but he had no choice.

It was decided to have a family supper and meeting at Kayla's, that night. They had much to discuss. Lou, Gabe, Samuel and Hawk left to do what they did best. Hunt a killer.

BETRAYAL

"The funeral will be tomorrow. The arrangements are all made," Jarod stated matter of factly once they had all arrived for supper.

After dinner, Lou cleared his throat, then said, "I have made my own arrangements. After the funeral, Hawk is going to escort Willow to Boston to stay with Janie until we catch Willard."

Willow looked up in shock at her husband's words. Only one word came out of her mouth, "No!"

Lou shook his head emphatically. "I am your husband; you will do as I say. I have to know you are safe, so I can do my job. I cannot constantly worry about your safety and concentrate on what needs to be done."

"I said no, Lou. I will not leave you." Tears filled her beautiful violet eyes. "You can't get rid of me. You *cannot* throw me away when I am inconvenient."

"Willow, you make me weak. Willard knows you are my weak link. He *knows* I cannot live without you. He knows I would not survive if something happened to you."

Willow stood, angry. "I make you weak? Have I not done everything you have told me? Have I disobeyed you one time?" She looked at all of them at the table. Every man was looking down at his coffee, including Samuel, the man who had always had her back.

"I see you all think I make Lou weak. Very well, I will leave right after the funeral." She threw her napkin down on the table and stood before wiping tears from her eyes with the back of her hand. " I don't have anywhere to go until then."

Lou held out his hand to her, but she pushed it away.

"I will not go anywhere with you. You are no longer my papa," she spat. "That takes trust, and you have broken it beyond repair." She turned her back to him as Jarod took her hand and he and Autumn led her from the restaurant to their home. Willow immediately ran to her room and slammed the door.

Hawk turned to Lou. "That went well," he said before he walked out the door after paying his bill, never looking back.

Samuel stood, and without a word, he did the same. That left Gabe, Missy and Ben.

Ben said to Lou, "Major would have protected her, you know, if you would have given him a chance. As it is, bring him back to me when she leaves. I will look out for him."

Missy threw her napkin on the table. "You, Lou, are an ass. I think I hate you." She started to walk out. Gabe gave Lou a shrug of his shoulders and hurried after his wife.

WILLOW STAYED IN HER ROOM. Autumn and Wynter had both tried to get her to come out for breakfast, but she would not open the door.

Finally, after everyone else had gone, Storm knocked on the door.

"Willow, I will walk you home. Lou has left for the office. You can pack your things and put on a pretty dress for ole Roger's funeral. It's just the service at the church. They will bury him as soon as the ground thaws.

The door opened a crack and a sad little face peeked out. Storm gave her a friendly smile, holding out his hand for her.

She opened the door and stepped out. "Thank you for escorting me so I can pack."

Back at her house, Willow pulled out some of her older clothes. She would leave her sexy nighties and her pretty dresses behind. She knew in her heart she would not return. Her heart was too broken. Giving Storm her trunk to carry to Autumn's, she chose a nice but plain dress to wear to the church. Before they left, she took off her wedding ring and set it on the table. Wiping her eyes, she turned to follow Storm. She locked the door, standing in the doorway before pulling it closed for just a minute. Looking over the home she had loved and all the love that once was in it, she saw all the little loving touches she had put into it—the curtains and tablecloth, the crocheted afghan on the sofa. She firmly shut the door for the last time. In the church, she sat alone. Lou came to sit next to her, but she scooted as far from him as she could and left as soon as the service was over. She never said a word to her husband as Hawk led her to the wagon that would take them to the train station. She had left her family and friends and the only home she had ever known without a word of goodbye to anyone.

Once they arrived at Fort Kearney and the train, Hawk saw to the loading of their trunks. The two-day train ride did nothing to lift Willow's spirit. She picked at her food and ate very little, preferring to stay in their car and watch out the window as they traveled further away from her home. Hawk found her sitting up in the seat next to the window both mornings. She had not been to bed. Instead, she had dozed here and there for most of the trip. She spoke very little, preferring her own company. She felt betrayed by all the men, including Hawk. They all had let her down when she needed them the most. She had a secret she dared not share. She was sure she was two months pregnant. She also knew she would raise her child by herself. It broke her heart that her child would be raised without his father. She was raised in an orphanage. She knew what it felt like to feel unwanted. She knew she would give this child all the love any child could ask for.

Once they arrived at the Boston station and the train conductor announced they were unloading, she looked out the window. She had never met Janie, Jarod's sister, before, but he had described her perfectly. She recognized the little woman with the brown hair and bright blue eyes right away, along with her big strong husband, Adam. Their children were in their early teens, and every one of them looked loved and well cared for.

Abel, the oldest boy, took Willow's trunk, and along with Hawk, they carried it to the waiting carriage.

Abigail held out her hand to Willow. "I am Abigail, and this is my sister, Sarah. We are pleased to meet you."

Janie looked on with pride at her family before she turned to Willow and added, "Welcome to our home, Willow. Please follow me to our carriage. Our home in an hour's drive away from town."

Everyone climbed in the carriage but Abel and Hawk. Hawk had brought his big roan. He pulled Abel up behind him. The carriage driver asked where they wanted to go and once he was told, off they went.

Once they arrived, Hawk and Abel again carried Willow's trunks into the house. Willow looked around in awe. Jarod had told her that Adam was in architecture, but this house was more beautiful than she could have imagined. The two-story home had a large entryway. When she walked into the living room, she was amazed at the intricate woodwork and the huge fireplace. The carpets were soft and cushy to walk on. The room was done in warm color, and the windows went from the floor to the ceiling, facing the side of the house with the large flower garden and immaculate lawn.

Janie laughed at her expression. "We needed a big enough home for the kids, you see. Let me take you to the bedrooms upstairs, so you can rest before supper. We can talk more once you have rested."

Willow agreed; she had not slept well on the train and the ride to this beautiful home had lulled her.

Janie showed her a large room at the end of the hallway. The children each had their own rooms in the middle, and Janie and Adam had a large bedroom identical to the one they offered Willow. There was a water closet in the hallway for the children and one in each of the end bedrooms. There were two bathrooms downstairs. Janie explained that when there are three children in the house, more than one was needed. The bedroom was beautiful, too. The carpets kept the floors warm and the fireplace was full of wood, the flames dancing merrily. The windows were large and had curtains to match the bedspreads. Willow's window overlooked the large back yard. She could see the tire swing hanging off the large oak tree. The stables were farther back.

"I will send Henrietta up to you before supper. She will help you hang your clothes or dress. She is very good with hair. We don't have many servants, but the ones we have you can trust implicitly. Milo will bring up more wood, once we go down for supper. William works in the stable, in case you have a need to ride. Jerimiah and Warren are our field hands. They grow and make the hay and harvest the oats for the horses and our cattle. Sharon is our cook, and that does it."

Willow sat on the bed, enjoying the softness, and before Janie left, she was lying on the quilt sound asleep. Janie smiled as she took the afghan from the sofa and covered her, kissing her on the cheek before she left.

Hawk was downstairs explaining everything that couldn't be explained in a telegraph.

Janie sighed. "No wonder she looks so sad. No matter, we will keep her busy. I have set up a job interview in two days' time with Alexander, the head of one of the most prestigious hospitals in Boston. He and his wife, Lavonne, happen to be very good friends of ours and very good people. He has agreed to interview Willow. Between that and the impeccable references Jarod sent him, she is a shoo in for a very good job."

Hawk smiled; this family was exactly what Willow needed. "Her husband will come for her when we have captured Willard. "

"If she has made a life for herself here, he will have to win her back now, won't he?"

Adam shook his head at his wife. She had a bad habit of sticking her cute little nose in other marriages. He knew it was because she was so happy with her marriage, but from time to time, he had to curb her inclinations. The threat of a good spanking usually calmed her down.

"Janie, that is enough. It is not our concern. Our concern is to see that she is happy while she is with us and to make sure she is protected."

His warning did not go unnoticed by either Hawk or Janie. A rosy blush crept up her cheeks as Hawk smiled in amusement. This family was adorable, the children well behaved, and Adam and Janie were plainly in love.

Adam smiled at her embarrassment; the blush always warmed his heart. He bent down to taste her lips and the blush deepened, bringing a chuckle to his lips.

She cleared her throat and changed the subject. "Your room is down here in the spare room next to the water closet. I will let Adam show you where. You have time to take a bath or to rest before supper. I will see how soon Sharon will have it ready. If you will excuse me, boys?"

Janie left for the kitchen. Sarah and Abbey were in the kitchen helping Sharon make the cookies. Janie laughed at Sarah. Her face had chocolate on it from the frosting. At nine, she was the youngest, spoiled to a fault by everyone in the household. Abbey was busy learning when to take them out of the oven. Sharon was very good at teaching the girls how to cook. Abbey was becoming quite a cook, even at her age. Abel followed Adam everywhere he could. Janie was so proud of her family.

The next morning, bright and early, Janie and Willow went into town to meet Alexander. As they entered the huge modern hospital, Willow couldn't help but peek into some of the rooms. The rooms were spacious and cheerfully painted. She begged Janie to take her to the children's ward, where she was amazed at the children sitting up and playing board games. The rooms had princes and princesses. The food on tables looked delicious and inviting. Many children were in their rooms sleeping or being cared for by nurses who talked to them in soft, kind voices. By the time they arrived at Alexander's office, Willow had her mind made up. She would work at being a children's nurse. She wanted it more than she ever imagined.

Janie knocked on Alexander's door, and he bid them to enter, a smile crossing his face when he saw Janie. Standing, he held his hand out to her. "Janie, it is so nice to see you. I see you brought your lovely guest. Let me see," he tapped his finger on his lips, thinking, "it is Willow, is it not?"

Willow smiled and held out her hand to him. "Yes, sir, it is. I would very much like to work in the children's ward, sir. Please give me a chance. I will work hard for you and learn as much as I can."

Alexander chuckled as he sat down and bid the girls to do the same. He opened a folder he had sitting off to the side.

"Jarod gave you a raving recommendation. Did you know Jarod's father was a good friend of mine?" He smiled as he thought about the good ole days. "Yes, I sure missed Steven when he left for Wyoming. When can you start, young lady?"

Willow clapped her hands in excitement. "Tomorrow, sir. I promise I won't let you down."

Alexander smiled at the excited young girl. He didn't know what had caused her to be so far from home, but he knew she was in a good place. Janie and her husband were very good people.

"How about you come see me first thing in the morning, and I will get you all set up with a uniform. And you said you would like to work in the children's ward, hmm? Let me see what I can do, today, and I will let you know, tomorrow. Also, I have made it a rule that any young lady who starts at my hospital must have supper with me and the wife on Friday. Is that also agreeable to you?"

Willow laughed for the first time in a long while. "Of course, sir, although I doubt it is a rule. I would be happy to come to dinner. I will have to ask Janie to bring me tomorrow." She looked over at her new friend, who was also excited and happy.

"That won't be necessary, young lady. I will have a carriage pick you up and drop you off at home when work is finished. Also, we have small apartments for the help if they live further away. You may choose one from the several that happen to be open. They are right at the back of the hospital. You may have your own apartment, which allows you to be close but still have time off to yourself on your days off. Is that something that you would be interested in? Food and furnishings are your own responsibility, of course, but I am sure we have some furniture in the attic we are not using. I will talk to Lavonne about it, tonight. Let's give it a week or two and we will talk again. In the meantime, I will see you tomorrow and for dinner, Friday." He stood as the girls did and held out his hand again. "Very nice meeting you, Willow, and I hope you feel you can come to me if you have any problems."

After they arrived at their carriage outside, Willow was so excited, she squealed in delight, turning in a circle, her arms hugging herself.

"Oh, Janie, I am so happy I have begun my new life already."

Janie looked at her with concern. "Willow, do not be in such a hurry to leave us. Please give it a week or two before you decide. This is a big decision."

"I know, Janie, and you and your family have been very good to me, but I don't like to be beholden to others. I will wait a week or two, but I long to work in the children's ward. That is the work I have always loved at home, working with the children. I have wanted to have children of my own for so long." She looked down at her feet. She hated to lie to Janie and her family, but she would not take the chance that she would tell Jarod or force her to go back home to Lou.

"You were an orphan, too, weren't you? Just like my children. I hope they don't feel like they have to leave us too soon. I love them as if they were my own."

"I never had a ma or a pa, even an adopted one. I learned to do for myself until Jarod and Samuel made me part of their family." The smile returned to her face. "I cannot wait until tomorrow."

When they arrived home, Janie told Hawk the news as Willow went upstairs to change into an older dress. She still didn't talk to Hawk. She just wanted him to go home.

Hawk laughed as Janie told him of Willow's excitement. "I am so happy for her. Even though I did not agree with Lou to send her away, it was his right as her husband to protect her any way he thought best. I am afraid she blames us all for abandoning her when she needed our support. I hope Lou doesn't wait too long to come and get her, or he may find himself without a wife."

"She could easily have a life she has always dreamed of, right here," Janie agreed. "Alexander offered her one of the apartments they have out back of the hospital for staff. They are very nice homes."

"I will be leaving tomorrow on the first train home. Best I go to town and see about a ticket. Janie, thank you for taking care of Willow while Lou sorts this out. I am hoping we can catch this bast…er…man, sooner, rather than later."

With that, Hawk walked to his room to pack his things, and then he would ride to town for his train ticket. He was happy that Willow had found a job and happiness so soon. He would relay the message. Samuel would be happy, also.

At supper that night, Willow was so excited, she could barely sit still.

"I would get a scolding if I was squirming around like that at supper. Wouldn't I, Mama?" Sarah asked innocently.

"Sarah, that is none of your affair. Kindly mind your own plate,"

Janie scolded her daughter. Sarah got a pout on her face until she saw Adam looking at her seriously. She began immediately eating again. "Yes, Mama."

Willow tried to settle down after that. She didn't want to get the children in trouble. "Yes, I am very excited to be working with children again."

Hawk looked up from his plate. "I am glad you will be happy, little one. If you need anything, please don't be afraid to telegraph us and let any of us know."

Willow looked him right in the eye and said, "I don't ever want to have to talk to any of you again, much less ask any of you for help. I don't want to give any of you any false hope that I have or ever will forgive you." She put her fork down and left the table for her room.

Adam rose to go after her, but Hawk put up his hand to stop him, "I don't blame her. She is hurting and feeling betrayed by the people she loved. Let her be for a while. Maybe in time, she will forgive us. Let her go for now."

Adam looked at Hawk for a minute before he nodded and sat back down. Sarah watched her father closely. He was still angry but accepted what the big Indian said. For now.

The next morning, the carriage arrived right on time. Hawk was saddling his own horse to leave for the train station. His trunks were in the carriage with Willow. She was glad he was leaving. He was a reminder of what she had left behind, and she wanted to look to the future.

The carriage driver first followed Hawk to the train station, and after Hawk took his trunk out of the carriage, he looked at Willow. She could see sorrow in his eyes.

"Little one, I know you don't understand now, but please know we have always loved you and only want you safe and happy." He reached over to squeeze her hand.

She pulled her hand back. "Safe travels, Hawk. Please tell

everyone not to worry about me. I am a survivor and will be just fine on my own. I have Janie and Adam to watch over me."

Hawk sadly nodded before he took the reins of his horse and walked to the carriage to load him and see him fed and comfortable before he entered their private car. Soon enough, the train whistle blew and began slowly pulling away.

Willow wiped the tears from her eyes.

A NEW LIFE

*A*s soon as Willow entered the hospital, an older nurse led her to Alexander's office again.

He stood looking at the sad girl. Something was hurting her. He knew it was not his affair, but he had come to care already for the little woman who had been so enthusiastic yesterday. He offered her his hand as he led her to the chair in front of his desk.

"I have found you a place in our infants' ward, taking care of sick babies. Is that something that would interest you, Willow? It's right next door to the children's ward and you would be welcome to visit any time you would like, of course."

Willows eyes lit up. "That would be really nice, sir."

"I have also found three apartments you may choose from at the end of the week if you choose to stay with us. That is up to you, of course."

"I would love that. I love being with Janie and Adam, of course, too, but I have been on my own for a long time and prefer it."

"You will be supervised by a matron, of course; you know that. No men in the rooms." He held up his hand as she began to protest. "I know I don't have to worry about you, but I have to let you know the rules, at any rate. No drinking or smoking. There, it is said. Now, are you still interested?"

Willow eagerly nodded her head. "Yes, sir, and the sooner the better."

"Yes, well, we will wait a week and see if you are still happy here. Now, my head nurse in the nursery is Mrs. Wyler. She will escort you to the uniform room, so you can pick out a couple of uniforms that will fit you. She will then take you to the nursery and introduce you to the other nurses and your charges. And, I'll see you Friday at six sharp. I'll send a carriage to you at Janie's home to pick you up and deliver you home again. Is there anything else I have forgotten? Oh, yes, your pay will be two dollars a week, with a raise in thirty days. Is that acceptable?"

Willow eagerly nodded again. "I don't care about the money, sir, not now, at least. I have brought enough to last me a few months."

Alexander rose just as Mrs. Wyler knocked on the door.

A few minutes later, Willow followed her down the hall as the woman explained all the rules and her duties to her.

THE WEEK FLEW BY. Willow worked hard and worked every extra hour when she was asked to do so. The head nurse was very pleased with her; she learned fast and was dependable. Friday came, and Willow was given a half day off to get ready for her dinner with Alexander and his wife, Lavonne. She spent a couple of hours shopping for a nice dress to wear. While she was selecting the dress, the matching hat caught her eye. She hated to spend the extra money, but it was so pretty that she couldn't pass it by. As she counted her money, she happened to see some penny candy. She decided the children deserved a treat, so she purchased enough for all them, also. She had the carriage driver load her boxes, and in no time, they were headed home. The carriage driver was to wait for Willow and return her to Alexander's home. Willow showed him the servants' door and Sharon gave him some supper while he waited.

Willow took her time dressing. She wanted to look nice for her first dinner with the head of the hospital. She asked Henrietta to dress her hair and pin her hat on at just the right angle. As she looked in the mirror, she couldn't believe how much she was looking forward to meeting Lavonne and spending the evening with her and Alexander.

When she came down the stairs, she heard Adam give her a whistle. "You look beautiful, Willow."

Janie stood beside him with a smile and a twinkle in her eyes. "You sure do. I hope you have a good time, and we will see you home about tenish, then. I will wait up; I want to hear all about it. And, you said you have tomorrow off, so I will let you sleep in." She walked up to give Willow a kiss on the cheek.

Willow hummed as she walked out to the carriage. The driver helped her up, and she sat comfortably for the entire ride to the Walters' home, enjoying the warmth of the carriage and the well-sprung ride.

As she was escorted in, she looked in awe around at the mansion. Massive pillars lined the front porch. She had never been in such a large, fancy home. Inside, the décor was warm and inviting. Large pictures of what Willow was sure were distant family members hung on the walls in the entryway. The carpet was plush and a warm cream color. The fireplaces were huge and had fires blazing in them, making the rooms all toasty.

She was led to a waiting room, and in a very short amount of time, an older woman dressed elegantly came in to introduce herself.

"I am Lavonne, Alexander's wife. You must be Willow. I have heard nothing but good things about you. Please be seated; Alexander will be down soon. Dinner will be in a very few minutes." The woman smiled welcomingly. "While we wait, why don't you tell me about yourself?"

Willow explained that she was an orphan who had worked to get her nursing degree. She excitedly told Lavonne how happy she was working in the nursery, but when it came time to tell her about Lou, she felt she didn't have the heart.

"My husband is a detective. He sent me away to Janie and Adam's to keep me safe until he could dispose of a very bad man who had been threatening all of us."

Lavonne looked at her carefully. She could see this woman was unhappy

"Why were you the only one in the family sent away?" She was confused.

Tears formed in Willow's eyes. "He said I made him weak, that the bad men knew I was the weak link and they could use me to hurt him," she whispered. She wiped the tears from her eyes and looked at the older woman. She took a deep breath and added, "Please don't feel sorry for me. I am determined to find a new life. One that will make me happy. Working in the nursery is a dream come true for me. It is a beginning."

Lavonne was amazed at Willow's strength and had nothing but respect for the young woman.

She patted Willow's hand. "I don't feel sorry for you, Willow. I am in awe of your strength. That is not saying you have to travel on this journey alone. We will help you all we can. Not because you are weak, but because you have earned it."

Just then, Alexander came into the room and dinner was called. They went into a beautiful dining room and had a very lovely meal.

Alexander asked Willow if she had decided to take an apartment, and when she told him she was interested, he suggested Lavonne meet her at the apartments.

"You two can decide which one suits you the best, and Lavonne can show you some of the furniture we have in the attic and you can choose what you like. Why don't you girls go tomorrow? It's Saturday and you have the weekend off. It will be a good time to get it done. I will have some of the help give you a hand with moving the furniture."

The next day, Willow skipped down the stairs as Adam and Janie were just finishing breakfast.

When she mentioned her plans, Janie was worried that Willow was making too many decisions too quickly. "Willow, are you sure you are not rushing into something you will regret later?"

Willow shook her head and said, "No, Janie, thank you for all your hospitality, but I am ready to be on my own." One of the reasons she wanted to be on her own was that she wanted to hide the fact she was pregnant from Janie and her family as long as possible. She was afraid when they found out, they would tell Lou. She had a few mornings already when she had felt nauseous.

Adam stood and commented, "Then, we will help you all we can. I will have Milo and Jerimiah get the wagon ready and help to load your trunks and a few things you can have to make your new home feel more like a home."

"Don't worry, Adam, I just need my trunks, Lavonne has given me all the furniture I could ever want. It is a two bedroom with a lovely kitchen and a large living room. I will make my own curtains and crochet my own sofa covers and make a quilt for the bed. In the meantime, I have everything I need."

Janie and Adam gave her a hug as she pulled away in the carriage with her trunks, later that morning.

When she arrived at her new home, she could see Lavonne's men were already at work. No one knew, but she would fill the second bedroom with baby things. She wasn't sure she could stay with a baby, but she would cross that bridge when she came to it. She and Lavonne spent the day arranging furniture with the aid of some of their help, and when it came suppertime, they arranged to meet Alexander at one of the better restaurants in the area.

She spent the next day enjoying her new home and dreaming about how she would decorate the baby's room.

The week after that went quickly, with Willow working hard

and long hours. She grew attached to the little mites in her charge. Then, one night, she got word that one of her littlest babies, one who was born too early, was in trouble. The child was fighting for her little life. A specialist was trying to help her, and Willow did all she could to assist, but it was all in vain. She watched as the life left the baby's eyes. When the doctor pulled the blanket over the infant's face, he turned to her with tears in his eyes.

"We have the grim duty to tell the parents. They are in the waiting room. Would you join me? It is one job I have never gotten used to."

Willow agreed, even though her own heart was breaking.

A BABY SURPRISE

She held the mother as the doctor explained to the father that God had taken his little one home. She had just been too small to survive. The father had tears in his eyes as Willow relinquished the mother into her husband's arms.

The doctor thanked Willow and escorted her home before he left for his own house. Willow sat alone, feeling drained and overwhelmed. She hugged the stuffy she had bought for her own baby and cried. She needed a papa right now—someone to hold her and rock her and tell her he would always be there when she needed him. But she didn't have anyone like that in her life anymore. She hugged the stuffy and rocked herself on the sofa. The tears were falling faster and faster as her hand went down to her tummy, to her own baby. She was alone. No matter how many friends she had, she was still alone. She no longer had a papa. She would have to be strong on her own, but she didn't know if she was strong *enough*. The baby needed a father, too, not just a working mother. But she would not go back to making Lou weak. Being the weak link was the last thing she or her baby needed. Her thoughts went back and forth as she sat and cried all alone. Finally, exhausted, she went to bed with the stuffy, and her thumb found its way into her mouth as she fell asleep.

The next morning, she felt nauseous as soon as she opened her eyes. Running for the water closet, she knelt down and tried to throw up what wasn't there to begin with. Her head hurt from lack of sleep and crying. She crawled back into the bed and fell back to sleep and that was where the matron who was sent to look for her found her. The woman felt her head and immediately ran for Alexander.

"She has a fever; I think she needs the day off to rest. She has been putting in too much overtime. She is exhausted, poor child. I will look in on her later, but I think she needs sleep."

Alexander agreed, but before the matron left, he called for the head nurse at the nursery. When he got the whole story about Willow's night, he understood. He scolded the head nurse, telling her she was taking advantage of Willow's willingness to work.

"No more overtime until I give the green light." The head nurse agreed, and the matron left for her duties.

Willow slept the whole day, only getting up to go to the bathroom and take a drink of water. By the next morning, it was evident she was going to be plagued by morning sickness. She made herself some peppermint tea and ate toast for breakfast before she headed off to work. She needed some overtime to make up for yesterday, but when she asked to work it, she was told she was not allowed until it was approved by Alexander.

She walked to his office, nervously wondering if she needed to apologize. When she was bid to enter, she could see he was sitting back in his chair looking her over carefully.

"How do you feel, Willow?"

"I am fine, sir, I just needed a little rest."

"I came to check on you yesterday and you were sound asleep with a stuffy. You looked so childlike and cute." He stopped to think before he spoke again, treading carefully with his words. "I have noticed you have been gaining a little weight, Willow, and I saw that you had been sick. Are you, by chance, pregnant?"

Willow immediately shook her head until she saw him watching her carefully. "Yes, sir, almost three months now."

"And, Willow, does Janie or Adam or the father know?"

"No, sir, the father said I make him weak. I didn't think he would want a child now. It would also make him weak, would it not?"

"Sit down, child, I won't bite you. I only mean to help you. Don't you think the father has a right to know? If he did wrong by you, doesn't he have the right to try to fix it?"

Willow shook her head. "No, sir. He betrayed me. Lou and the rest of them threw me away when I became a weak link. I don't trust them anymore."

"Willow, I understand that they hurt you. They hurt your feelings and your pride, but you must think of the baby. I've come to love you like my own child. As my child, I would tell you that you are not being fair to yourself or the baby. Let the man have his say. Then, if he throws you away, I would ask you to live with us. Lavonne has always wanted children, but after we lost the first one, she was never able to have any more. You are like a daughter to us. We would take care of you and the baby. But first, the father must have a chance to make amends."

Willow stood. "No, if I can't trust him, the baby will not be able to, either."

Alexander stood, too. "I will let Janie and Adam know; they are your family here in Boston. They'll know what to do."

"I'll run away, and no one will find me."

Alexander laughed at that. "Little girl, have you forgotten who the father is? Who the grandfather is? You will never be able to hide from these men. Go to your apartment, and I will talk with Janie and Adam. We'll go from there. I will tell you now, if you try to run away, I will do what any father would do if his child disobeyed him.

Ask Lavonne; I can give a spanking you will not soon forget. Do you understand me, little one?"

Willow nodded. "This is my baby. Not yours," she sobbed.

"It is the father's baby, also. Let us do what is best for you. I know you want to do this all on your own, but you can't. Your baby and you will both suffer."

When Willow left for home, Alexander sat down, deep in thought. His fingers steepled as he decided on a plan of action. First, he wrote a note to Adam, who was working in town. After he explained to Adam the situation and Adam came to see him, he asked him, "Does her husband love her, Adam? Do you know?"

"Hawk and I talked before he left for home. He said Lou loved her dearly, but he was so afraid for her that he was not getting sleep. He was having nightmares. He said some things he should not have said, but he was doing what he thought best for Willow. These men who were after the family were targeting Willow. They were very bad men."

Alexander nodded, accepting what Adam had said. He replied, "Well, we need to let Jarod know what is going on. He will have to come up with a solution. In the meantime, I will put Willow on a restricted schedule. If she has morning sickness, she need not come to work until she is feeling better—and no overtime. She is working too many hours, and my thought is she is trying to forget someone."

Adam nodded at the comment. "She doesn't need the money, but I think she doesn't want to touch any of her money. I think she is trying to work herself into exhaustion, so she can forget the man she loves. He has made a holy mess of things, but I am sure he loves her and thought he was doing what was best for her. I will telegraph Jarod." He stood and held out his hand to Alexander. "Thank you for keeping an eye on Willow and for letting me know there was a problem."

Alexander shook his hand with enthusiasm as he said, "Lavonne and I love her, too. Let me know how things are going. Keep me informed, will you? I will also keep in touch with you."

Adam hurried to the telegraph office and sent off a message to Jarod. He wanted it done before he went home. He knew Janie would have her own ideas about how things should go. When he got home, he informed her of the situation.

Janie was ecstatic at the news and wanted to see Willow immediately, but Adam stopped her.

"She has just been found out, Janie. Let her have some time to think. I believe Jarod will be here in a few days to confront her. Give her some time."

∽

IN THE MEANTIME, Willow had started working in the nursery again on a restricted schedule. The days went by slowly, but the work was rewarding. It gave her some much-needed time to think.

It had been four days since Adam had telegraphed Jarod. He had finally received the reply. It was as he expected. Jarod would be on the next train to Boston. They were hoping he would bring Autumn, but he understood that she was home, helping Wynter with the triplets. Jarod would arrive on Saturday. He hurried home to tell Janie.

Janie was so excited to hear the news of Jarod coming. It had been a long while since she had seen her brother. She began making the preparations immediately.

Then, Adam returned to town and work, after stopping off and talking to Alexander and then Willow.

Willow answered the door as soon as she heard the knock. She had taken a small nap after dinner and was just getting ready to go back to the nursery. While she was starting later in the morning, she stayed in the nursery until supper. When she saw that it was Adam at the door, she knew Jarod would be in Boston soon.

Adam confirmed her worse fear, to which she informed him, "I am not going home with him, Adam. I refuse to be bounced around at their convenience. I am making a life for myself here. I love my job and Alexander and Lavonne. He cannot just come back here and disrupt my life again."

"All he is asking is the chance to talk to you, whether here or Alexander's home or at a restaurant with many people around. He just wants to talk to you. May I make a reservation for all of us at the Parker House? I can get a private room and we can dine and discuss this…er…problem with Jarod."

"It is not Jarod's problem. It is mine and mine alone. I have been doing fine on my own. They didn't want me. I will not be moved like a piece of furniture. I have a career here."

"But what of the baby, Willow? What kind of life will he have without a father? Oh, I know he will have me and Alexander, but it is not the same as a father. The other children will make fun of him and he will struggle. What about the baby? Can you not give Lou a chance to make this right? Willow, the man loves you. He only wanted what he thought was best for you, your safety. He made a mistake, yes, but is a man not allowed to make a mistake? Should a mistake cost him his wife and son or daughter? Can you not at least hear what Jarod has to say?"

Willow turned so Adam did not see the tears slide down her cheek, but he had seen. He turned her into his chest as he held her. He led her to the settee and sat, pulling her down on his lap. He handed her his kerchief to wipe her eyes. She thought of all the times Lou had held her on his lap when she had cried. She began to cry harder at the memory and the hurt in her heart the memories brought.

"Willow, we don't want to hurt you. That is the last thing we want, but you have to know that Lou loves you. You know it in your heart. I think if you allowed yourself to think on it, you would also admit that you love him. Let me make a reservation at the Parker House. Let us—you, Janie, Jarod, and me talk this over like adults." He rocked her while she struggled with her tears.

"All right, Adam, make the reservations, I will meet with Jarod. I will not make any promises."

"That is all I ask, Willow. Just listen to what the man has to say."

It was decided that the dinner should take place Sunday night to give Jarod time to rest.

Sunday afternoon, Willow had laid out the clothes she planned on wearing and had taken a long hot bath. She was too nervous to eat much of a lunch, so she just nibbled on toast with her tea.

Lavonne had come over and helped her with her hair.

"Is there anything you need right now, Willow? Do you need a mother to talk to? Do you have any questions?"

Willow looked at the woman whom she had admired for all these weeks. "No, Mama. I am ready, I think. I will not let Jarod bully me into leaving if I am not ready. I would happily stay here with you and Alexander. I am beginning to love the life I am building here, but I know it's not fair to you or Janie to put the burden of helping to care for this child."

"Oh, Willow, do you not know, by now, we love you like a daughter? It would not be a burden at all. Both Janie and I know what it is like not to have a child of our own. Janie has found hers, but I have not."

Willow could see Lavonne's bottom lip wobble as she tried to fight the tears.

"Lavonne, please do not cry. I cannot bear to see you so unhappy." She rushed over to put her arms around her friend.

Lavonne smiled then. "You must do what you think is best for you and the baby. Do not let me interfere in your decision. I have heard the father of this child loves you. You must consider that."

As the time drew near, Willow considered what she would tell Jarod. The buggy stopped in front of her apartment just as Lavonne left for home. The driver got down and put down the step for her to enter. She spent the journey to the hotel in contemplation.

She was met at the door by Adam and Janie. Janie did not look happy, but Adam gave her a stern look that let her know he was watching her. They were seated in a private room, and water was brought as they waited for Jarod.

Janie looked at Willow and then Adam before she seemed to decide she needed to tell Willow something. "Willow, Jarod did not come alone."

Willow looked up and Janie continued. "Samuel and Suzy and Hawk and Little Bird also came." Before she could say more, in walked the five of them. A more impressive group of people would never be found. The men all filled the doorway as the two women stood in front of them. As soon as they saw Willow, the women rushed over to her with arms outstretched.

Suzy gave Willow a gentle hug. "Oh, Willow, we have missed you so much."

Little Bird gave her a hug next. "We are so glad to be able to come and see you, little one."

A smile tugged at Willow's lips before she turned to bump into Samuel, who had waited his turn for a hug. He bent down and gave her a kiss on top of her head before he relinquished her to Hawk. Jarod was the last to give her a hug before they all were seated. The waitress brought them all coffee, promising to return with menus for everyone.

Samuel started, "Well, little one, did you know you were pregnant before you left us? Did you feel you couldn't tell us?"

Suzy slapped Samuel on the arm. "Samuel, have some manners. Don't you remember that she didn't want to leave? You men practically forced her."

"That was a mistake that will never be repeated," Samuel stated manner of factly.

Hawk spoke up quickly, agreeing, "We promise you now, little one, this will never happen again."

Willow said, "I don't want to come back with you. I have begun to make a life for myself here. I learned I cannot depend on anyone for my happiness but myself."

Suzy shook her head as she looked at Willow, reaching over to take her hand. "Willow, I know how hard you have worked for your career, but I promise you now, no one will take it away from you. Jarod has promised to add a nursery at the new hospital that is being built. You will be in charge. The family has discussed it. Alexander has told us how happy you were working in the nursery. We are willing to add a nursery wing to the hospital. We just want you to be happy."

"We will all help with the baby when the time comes, so you can feel free to work at the hospital whenever you want," Little Bird added.

Willow looked at her friends before she sadly shook her head. "You cannot guarantee me anything. Lou is my husband. Didn't you tell me, Samuel, that I had to come to Boston because Lou was my husband and he decided? He had all the say?"

Samuel looked at Willow sadly. "That will never happen again, Willow. We will never abandon you again. No matter what. That is my promise to you."

Willow knew Samuel's word was his bond. She also knew these men, and to some extent, the women had betrayed her when she needed them the most. The only difference was the baby.

"I think the only reason you all want me to come home is because of the baby. I don't think if it was just me, any of you would be here."

She heard the gasp behind her. She knew instantly who was standing there.

She put her hands over her mouth as she turned to see Lou, his mouth a perfect "O," his eyes open wide. He knelt down beside her, looking into her violet eyes. "You are having a baby? Willow, you didn't tell me?" He looked around at everyone gathered at the table. "None of you told me?" He looked so hurt.

Willow didn't know what to say, but she was not ready for this. Adam and Janie had now betrayed her. Adam had lied to her.

She stood to leave, but Lou stopped her. "I didn't know about the baby, Willow. I came to talk to you. I know I made a terrible mistake by sending you away. I should have protected you at home. My biggest mistake was opening my big mouth and telling you that you made me weak. The fact is you made me strong. I was weak without you. Gabe and Samuel found out where Willard was and tried to capture him. He fought them and was killed, but I couldn't be there. I couldn't think without you. I could only remember the feel of your arms around my neck when I held you, the scent of your hair, your skin, how soft your skin felt, and how your smile lit up my world. Fact is I can't live without you, Willow."

Tears streamed down her face as the man she loved apologized for the terrible, hurtful things he had said to her. He stood and took the chair next to her, pulling her into his lap. He held her close as he begged, "Please, Willow, give me a chance to make this up to you. I promise I will never send you away again."

Willow shook her head. Her heart was full, but this was too important to make a snap decision.

"I need to think about this. Let me ponder it for a day or two. I need some time alone." She turned to call a cab to take her home, but Lou took her elbow.

"I will escort you home, but first, let's order something to take home, so we can eat and discuss this—just the two of us. Please, Willow, give us a chance."

Willow agreed, and Lou ordered a very nice meal. They waited in the foyer for the food and then took a cab to Willow's apartment. When they arrived, she set the table.

"This is very nice. I know you love the life you have made for yourself here. It didn't take you long. I am proud of you, little one. You are not only an independent woman, but you are also smart. I also know you need a papa sometimes to hold you when the load becomes too heavy. You are not as vulnerable as you once were. Do you still want a papa, Willow?"

Willow looked at Lou and slowly nodded her head. "Sometimes I need it, Lou."

A smile crept across his face. "I love you, Willow. I always have and always will. Let's eat, and I will tell you about my dreams and why I felt I had to send you away. I don't want any secrets between us."

As they enjoyed their meal, Lou told her of the recurring dream.

"I have had them since I was a kid. Many times, they come true, but sometimes, I can alter them. I saw you in your yellow dress, the one I like so much." He stopped and looked at Willow with a smile before he continued. " I can't see who it is, but this man has his guns tied down. He is standing with you in front of him, his arm around your neck. Next, I see you lying in a pool of blood. I can't see the man, but I see your pretty yellow dress covered in blood. I couldn't shake the fear I had that I would lose you if I didn't send you out of harm's way."

Willow could see the sheen of tears in his eyes. This man was feared by many. He was a dangerous man, even to those big and strong, and not afraid of his own death. The fear of her death brought him to his knees. No one on this earth she knew of had ever seen Lou with tears in his eyes. No one had ever seen him with fear in his eyes. Willow saw it now. It broke her heart to see him so vulnerable.

"Lou, I love you, but I have to think about this for a spell. I have to think of what is best for our baby. If you reject our child like you did me, it will hurt him worse than it hurt me. I will not stand for it. Do you understand?"

"All I am asking for is a chance to fix this." He stood up and took his hat off the hook on the wall next to the door. "I will give you tomorrow. Then I am coming after what is mine." He quietly shut the door and left.

MAKING UP

It had been two days, and Willow had made up her mind. She had talked to Alexander and Lavonne. Even though she cared deeply for the director and his wife, she knew she needed to go home to her family. She had to give Lou another chance to make this right. Not just for the baby's sake, but for her own. Everyone had left her alone for two days, giving her the time to think. It was time to say goodbye to people who had been there for her when she'd needed them. She was just walking out the door, pulling her coat tighter against the wind, when she saw Samuel riding up to her door, his huge black horse plodding through the snow.

"Willow, Hawk says there is a big blizzard coming. We all need to get ready to be on the train, first thing in the morning. Nor'easters are nothing to fool around with, and according to Hawk, this one will follow us home. Please tell me you are coming with us. I am here to buy the tickets. The rest of the men are procuring rooms at the hotel. The train leaves at first light."

Willow nodded her head. "Yes, I am coming home with you. I will pack my bags right away."

"Thank the Lord, Willow. I will come back to help you, or I will send Lou back to help you load all the things you want to take back. We have our own cars, but please only bring what you need. If the storm is what Hawk is predicting, we may have to have most of it delivered after the storm. We may have to take just what the horses can carry."

"All right, please send Lou over to help me, and can you stop by the hospital after you buy the tickets, so I can talk to Alexander about the rest of my things?"

Samuel agreed and turned the horse to the train station and the ticket office.

It was not very long before Lou came by on his big brown horse. He hopped down and gave Willow a hard kiss, twirling her around. "Thank you, sweetheart, for giving us a second chance. I promise not to mess it up, ever again."

Willow smiled happily. "Come and help me pack what I need. Alexander should be here soon. I need to get the baby things all packed up, too."

Lou dug right in and helped her box all the things she would put on the train. "If we have to make a run for it, we will have it delivered as soon as the storm is over."

Willow packed her clothes, but when she came to the yellow dress, she turned to Lou and said, "I am going to leave this here. I won't buy any more yellow dresses, and maybe that will alter your dream."

Lou thought it was a good idea. He hired a wagon to put the trunks in and delivered them to their car that was waiting to be hooked up at the train station. They had four cars all their own. Each of the men had bought their own cars as soon as the train had allowed it. The cars were luxurious and roomy, private bedrooms and warm living quarters with plush seats to sit in and talk or just to look out the windows. That is the kind of luxury only the rich could afford. The cuisine in the dining car was always top quality. The passengers could eat in the dining car or have the food delivered to their car. Lou watched as they hooked the four of them up, all in a row, so the ladies could visit.

When the men were satisfied that all was in order, they went back to the hotel to have a light supper before they turned in early. Lou asked Willow to stay with him in his room. He wanted to be ready to leave at first light.

"I will sleep on the couch, if you prefer. I can take this as slow as you are comfortable with, Willow."

"I want us to get back to normal as soon as possible, Lou."

Lou smiled from ear-to-ear. "I am good with that, darlin'." It had been so long since he held his little Willow in his arms that he was having a hard time being patient. By the time everything was taken care of, it was suppertime. They all gathered for a nice meal together before an early bed.

Lou took Willow by the hand and led her to their room after supper, while the others watched with smiles on their faces, happy the two of them were willing to work on their problems.

When they entered the room, Willow opened her suitcase and retrieved the nightgown she had bought. It was made of a plain cotton, but it was pretty enough. Lou watched as she sat on the chair in front of the fire and took down her long, beautiful hair. She began to braid it, but Lou stopped her. He pulled her up and sat in the chair, placing her in front of him on the ottoman. He began to brush her hair. Long slow strokes, until it shone. He then began to braid it. He had done it many times in the past. When he was finished, he helped her up and into the bed.

He then began to undress slowly, until he stood like a half-naked god in front of her. He had left his long john bottoms on. She caught her breath as he moved to the bed. As he lifted the blanket, he crawled in and pulled Willow to his massive chest. "Her place," just over his heart. She stopped breathing for a second to hear his heart beat again. It lulled her to sleep.

Lou smiled as he gave her a gentle kiss on her forehead and pulled her even closer. He did not plan on having her tonight. He wanted to take this slow. He wanted to just hold her this first night. It had been so long since he had just held her. Tomorrow, on the train in their own car, he had plans to woo her. It would start first thing in the morning. He followed his wife into a deep sleep.

The next morning before the sun came up, Hawk was knocking on the door. "Time to get a move on."

Both Lou and Willow got up and got ready to begin their new journey. They all dressed warmly, had a hot breakfast, and while the men loaded the horses and saw to them, the women took care of the trunks. They were sitting in Hawk and Little Bird's car sipping coffee as the men entered.

"The engineer has said they are ready to leave. The snow that's coming is going to be a Nor'easter and they want to try and out run it to Kearney. We are going to have to decide when we get there whether to hole up and take a chance of being stranded or making a run for it. We have two days to decide, so I thought we could all meet in the dining car tomorrow, for lunch, and figure it out. In the meantime, enjoy our ride."

Lou grinned. "I have plans for Willow and me for dinner, so if you girls want to discuss things, feel free. After dinner, Willow belongs to me. Agreed?"

Willow blushed at the statement, but the other girls laughed. The men just smiled knowingly. The men went to the smoking car for a good cigar while the women sat and crocheted. Suzy gave Willow a bag with yarn she had left behind along with her crochet hooks. They began to chat.

"So, Willow, is everything getting better? Have you forgiven Lou for sending you away?" Suzy asked innocently, looking up from her crocheting to look at the younger woman.

"We are going to try to make it work. I love him, and if he loves me, it will work. I have missed him so much. Having said that, I will not be thrown away again."

Little Bird answered, "Did the men tell you they all had a

meeting and decided they would never let Lou, or anyone, ever do that again to any of you girls?"

"Yes, they did, and you know it, but I have a child to think of now."

Suzy squirmed in her seat. "I cannot wait for the baby. I have a secret, but I can't tell you until we get home. You will be very happy."

Little Bird nudged Suzy with her elbow. "You know you promised not to tell."

Willow looked at the women carefully. The smile on their faces told her they could not keep this secret. She looked at the door and then bent down to whisper, "I won't tell on you. I will act surprised. You know you both can't say stuff like that and not tell me."

Suzy looked to Little Bird, who nodded her head enthusiastically. "Missy is pregnant, too. The same as you, three months." Suzy squirmed again before she continued. "I promised to let her tell you, but I just can't wait. Please don't tell Samuel I told you. Don't tell Lou, either, 'cause he will tell Samuel and I will get a good spanking, and I am here to tell you it has been a while since I had one. I plan on keeping it that way."

Willow clapped her hands in glee. "Oh my gosh, Missy and I are expecting at the same time. Maybe we will have a Storm and Wynter situation." She hopped up and down in her seat until Little Bird put her finger to her lips.

"Shhh, the men will hear you."

Just then, Samuel opened the door to see what was going on, only to find them looking innocent, crocheting away. As soon as Samuel shook his head and closed the door, the women looked up from their work and laughed. That broke the ice; they began talking about home and what had happened since Willow had been gone.

Willow asked about Willard.

Suzy looked up at her, putting her crocheting down on her lap before she spoke. "They found him at the mayor's house. He had killed them both. It seems they were in prison in Yuma with the mayor's son. The one the boys put away for child trafficking. He had written his ma and pa asking them if a couple of friends of his could spend some time with them, if they would put them up until they got on their feet again. His pa had horses waiting for them all, thinking his son would escape with the other two, but Willard and Terry got into a fight with him and hurt him bad. That is how Terry got the scar. His father had bribed the cook to put some sleeping pills in the guards' food for their section. The men grabbed the keys and escaped, killed the mayor's men and stole the horses to escape. By the time they found the guards, it was too late. They were gone."

Willow gasped, waiting to hear the rest of the story.

"Lou was such a mess that Samuel made him stay in the office and do paperwork. He was making stupid mistakes. When Samuel and Gabe found out the boys spent time with the mayor's son, they rode over there, and lo and behold, there was Willard. He came out with a rifle, put it to his shoulder and pulled the hammer back. He missed Gabe by inches. Gabe had to shoot him," Little Bird finished.

Suzy took up the story again, "Lou wanted to come and get you right away, but then we got word that you were pregnant. The men decided it was best for him to find out from you about the baby. We left that decision to you."

Willow nodded her head, understanding more of the happenings.

LOU HAD LEFT the men in the smoking car, to take Willow for a short stroll to the dining car to see what it looked like. "Thought you would like to stretch your legs a bit," he said with a smile. His brown eyes had a twinkle in them that had Willow wondering what he was up to. When they got back to their car, it was lunchtime.

As Willow opened their door, she stopped and looked around in amazement. Inside was a candlelit dinner. The table setting was beautiful and the smells coming from under the silver dome made her mouth water. A waiter waited for them to enter before he removed the covers. He served them both the most tender of steaks and mashed potatoes and carrots in a glaze and, for dessert, a custard pie—not Lou's favorite apple pie, but Willow's favorite custard pie. The waiter served them, and after they enjoyed the most delicious meal, he took everything away, leaving them alone.

"Lou, that was beautiful." Tears formed in her eyes as she felt a warmness that had been missing for too long in her heart.

Lou gathered her in his arms and turned to lock the bedroom door before he sat her on the huge bed. Lou and the others had had their beds special made. He knelt down and kissed her as he began to unbutton her dress. Slowly, he slid it over her head and put it carefully on the dresser. He turned and lowered the straps on her slip, kissing first one shoulder and then the other. He slid them down until he uncovered his prize—her proud breasts, the nipples hard and waiting. He bent down and gave them each a gentle tug, twisting them as her nipples pebbled. He finished undressing her, standing up to just admire her beauty. Her stomach had a very slight bulge, her breasts slightly fuller, her thighs and legs firm from riding and working. Her bottom was full but not too full. Just right for spanking. He lay her down on top of the blankets so he could look his fill while he quickly pulled off his pants and shirt. Standing before her in all his glory, his manhood was sticking straight out, ready for her. As he lay next to her, she put his rod in her hand, touching it, pulling it gently.

"Aw, darlin', it has been too long; have mercy on a man." She just smiled as she continued pulling it and releasing it. Lou decided to take over. She would know, although he was repentant and willing to do anything for her at this stage, he was going to still be the leader in the family. He put a finger into her sopping pussy, then two, rubbing her button while sliding in and out. Her bottom came off the bed as a moan of pleasure left her plump lips. He knew he couldn't last long the first time. He crawled between Willow's legs and sunk himself all the way in while she let out a scream of ecstasy. He began to pump into his wife, all the way in and all the way out, harder and faster until her could feel her muscles tighten. His end wasn't far behind. They both reached it at the same time, coming apart together. Lou captured her last scream with a kiss before he rolled off, his breath coming in gasps. He took a second before getting up to clean them both and then crawling back into bed. He pulled her close.

"Let's take a nap, little one? We rose early this morn."

Willow nodded her head, halfway into a dreamless sleep already.

If anyone had asked either of them what happened that day, neither one would be able to tell them a thing. Love and sex and more was what the whole day and night consisted of. They skipped supper, so Lou could feast on his wife.

By morning, Willow was sore, so Lou had a hot bath brought in. While she soaked, he got out her brush and ribbons. He washed her hair and then the rest of her, stopping to suck on her nipples sticking out of the water, tantalizing him. He dried her and then brushed her hair until it was dry, before he braided it. Willow picked out a dress and finished while Lou took his turn in the now cool tub. When they were ready for lunch, they joined the rest of the smiling family in the dining car.

The men all had smirks on their faces until Lou looked at them all sternly and said, "It is not nice to stare; you do realize that? You are all being very rude."

The men all turned their attention to the menus in front of them. The women just had knowing smiles on their faces.

WE RIDE

*A*fter dinner, the men ordered a small glass of whiskey each while the women had coffee.

When everyone was settled, Hawk began, "The storm is close behind us. I am not sure we should try to make it from Kearney to home. It's a full day and night if we ride hard. We also have a pregnant woman with us and, of course, our women."

Samuel looked to the women and asked, "What do you think? Can you ride hard most of the way? Hawk says he knows a shortcut that will cut off four hours, but it's rough, and the snow already on the ground won't help matters any. We could stay at the hotel in Kearney, but with this size of a storm, it may be a while until we can even try to make it home. This is coming from Canada and it is going to be the worst we have seen in years, according to Hawk. He sees all the signs and says it is going to be bad."

Suzy and Little Bird decided they wanted to go home with the men.

Lou looked at Willow with concern. "There is nothing between Kearney and home. Farms and barns, but no town. If we leave Kearney, Willow, we have no choice; we have to complete the journey. Are you sure you are up to it?"

Willow looked conflicted, but Hawk added, "There is a cave on the shortcut about halfway from Kearney to home. If we hurry, we may...I say we *may*...have time to rest the horses and the women. It is a large cave, so we could light a fire and bring the horses in. We could make good time the rest of the way if we give the horses enough of a rest. Even an hour or two would help. We can tie an oat bag on the horses, so they can eat while we walk them. There's a pond in the cave. We may be able to break the ice, or we will have to melt some snow for them."

That convinced Willow. "I can do it, Lou, please let's go home. The baby hasn't hindered me yet."

Lou looked deep into her eyes before he made the final decision. "All right, little one. We ride. When we get to town, we will unload the horses and get them fed and watered and saddled while you girls find the nearest mercantile and get some sandwiches, jerky, and fruit, something we can eat in the saddle. We will ride as soon as you get back. I hope you are right on the timing, Hawk."

"Have I ever disappointed you, youngster?"

The women all laughed out loud as Lou answered his friend, "No, sir, never,"

Samuel spoke to Jarod. "Are you ready, my friend? This is not normal for you; will you be all right?"

Jarod just laughed and said, "I will be just fine. You seem to forget I am a little town doctor who sometimes rides hard for miles if an emergency warrants it."

Samuel nodded his head and slammed his hand on the table. "That's it, then. The conductor said we will arrive about sunrise. I am hoping the mercantile will be open. If not, let us know, girls, as soon as possible. We will wake the man, if need be. Let's meet for supper and then an early night." To Lou, as he glanced in Willow's direction, he added, "She will have a hard ride and will need to rest. You do realize that?"

Lou replied angrily, "I will take care of my wife. I realize the ride will be hard."

Samuel grunted his assent. Taking Suzy by the hand, he rose, as did the rest of the men.

Before he left the car, he warned, "Girls, only take what we really need. A change of clothes, mittens, hat, long johns. It will be cold, but we can't tire the horses. The rest, we will send for when we can."

The women all organized what they would take and what they would leave, while the men plotted the best and fastest way to go. It was an early supper and then bed.

Lou, Jarod, Hawk and Samuel stood in the smoking car, smoking cigars and looking out the window. Hawk was worried. The conductor said the train was going as fast as it could as they were trying to outrun the coming storm, too. Too much snow on the tracks made it damn near impossible for the train to go. They were all worried. The men finished their glasses of whiskey before they all left for their cars to retire for the night. The conductor promised to wake them an hour before they arrived.

When Lou got to his car, he found Willow sound asleep. A smile crawled across his face as he sat for a minute and just looked at her. She had her thumb in her mouth and looked simply adorable. He was so glad she had given him another chance to make this right. He would never send her away again. He had learned his lesson. He would stay and protect her. He crawled in and pulled her close until he, too, fell asleep.

Lou woke to the banging on the door. It was so warm and cozy in bed with Willow, he hated to get up, but he knew he had no choice.

"I am up. We will meet you in the dining car as soon as we can, " Lou yelled at Hawk as he continued to bang on the door.

Willow burrowed deeper into Lou's side. He hated to wake her. "Willow, hurry, we have to get up and dressed. A hot breakfast is waiting. It will probably be the last hot meal for a couple of days." He gave her a slap on her bottom, bringing a squeal from her.

She rolled over and sat up, her hair in disarray and sleep still in her eyes. He smiled down at her as he put on his pants and shirt.

Willow growled but got up and fumbled with her dress. Lou turned her around to button it for her. He handed her the brush and rushed to set their bag on the table.

They ate a hurried breakfast just as the sun rose over the hills. The men left the women to find food while they saddled and made sure the horses were fed and watered before the hard journey home. The morning air was freezing; they saw their breaths, and in no time, they were rubbing their hands. The women came running back with supplies to make cold sandwiches and also some jerky and fruit. The men carried their bags and hooked them on the saddles while they tied blankets to all the saddles. They made sure everyone had mittens and hats and scarves and their coats were buttoned up. Samuel went down the line, making sure all the saddles were on tight and the girls were all ready.

"We are going to start out at a good pace. I think it will be easier on Willow to gallop or walk and not trot. We'll start out fast and then walk some ways, then repeat it, until, hopefully, we get to the cave. When you girls notice your horses tiring, let us know. We will rest them by putting you up with us. Our horses are bigger and better capable of carrying two. We may need the horses rested the last part of the journey, if we have to make a run for it."

The girls all nodded that they understood, and they were off.

The bitter cold warmed some as the day wore on. Lou looked back and saw Willow slowing. She was tiring. When he came to take her up on his horse, she wanted to argue, but the look on his face told her it would do no good. He got out the blanket and wrapped it around both of them to keep more heat in before he took off again. Hawk and Samuel could see Suzy and Little Bird were still doing fine. Before they knew it, Willow was sound asleep in Lou's arms, snug and warm. The group kept a good pace until Suzy signaled her pony was lagging and needed a break. The girls climbed up on the men's horses as the men wrapped themselves and the women in blankets, the same as Lou had done with Willow.

Jarod led the girls' horses behind him. The lighter load gave them a much-needed break.

Hawk kept looking at the sky and checking the wind. They rode most of the day until they finally came to the shortcut Hawk had mentioned. It was slow and hard going, mostly hills, but they soon found themselves at the cave.

Jarod got down and tied the three horses before he lifted the girls down, one at a time.

Hawk tied his horse as soon as Little Bird was lifted down and went inside to find the dried wood he had left there the last time he had occasion to stay there. He began a fire as soon as possible and brought the horses in. He got out their feed sacks and tied them on each horse as he led them deeper into the cave. He then removed the saddles to offer them some relief. He had to break the crust of the small pond of water, but there was water underneath. As soon as the horses had their fill of feed, he led them to the water and gave them each a good rubdown. These horses would be the difference between life and death. The storm was coming fast. He had no doubt, now, they would have to make a run for home.

Samuel found a couple of rabbits and made quick work of skinning them and putting them over the fire. They would have a hot meal before they left, at any rate. The girls stayed near the fire to warm up.

Jarod and Lou found the rest of the wood, vowing to remember to bring some back and replenish the supply as soon as they could. The fire warmed most of the cave, and for an hour, they warmed themselves and took care of the horses. Hawk kept going outside nervously until he called Samuel over. The first snowflake was floating down.

"We have to go now. Hurry the girls up. The rest of us men will get the horses ready. We *cannot* get caught in this."

Samuel helped the women dress in warmed coats and hats and mittens, before putting out the fire.

Lou brought Willow's horse along with his. "I will let you ride your own horse until you start to slow us down, then you come with me." Willow agreed, and Lou helped her up, making sure she had on her mittens and hat.

Everyone was ready. They started out fast and didn't slow down much the first couple of hours. The snow was coming down harder and the wind had picked up speed. They had at least four more hours of hard riding. After a couple of hours, the men decided to rest the girls' horses as much as possible. They had the women climb up with them again. The huge Morgans could carry a load for a long way. Their strong legs chewed up the miles, never slowing. When their breath started coming harder, the boys slowed them and walked them for an hour. Hawk looked worried as the trail started to become snow covered. They didn't need to be slowed down because of slippery trails. The wind had picked up again, and the snow began to come down sideways, making it hard to see the trail or hear one another talk. The wind just whipped the words away.

Samuel stopped the group. "We have a good hour left until we reach home. I want you girls to get on your horses and ride beside us. We will each take a rope from your horses—not to slow us down, but so we know we have not lost anyone. If you girls cannot keep up, or your horses begin to tire pull on the rope hard, we will put you on our horses with us. Hopefully, that doesn't happen for a while. Each man is responsible for his own wife, but we must stick together. Jarod, I want you up here beside us. Does everyone understand? Give a yell or a tug on the rope if you need help."

Hawk looked at each of them and gave the order, "We ride." With that, he gave his horse a kick and they were off at a gallop. The horses were sure footed and galloped over the hills towards home. Their muscles were straining, but they never broke stride. After a half hour, the girls' horses began to lag behind. The men took their wives up with them and they again began to gallop, riding hard. If they didn't know the trail so well, they would have become lost. It was very hard to see it with all the snow. By the time they saw the lights of town below, they were still another half an hour away, the great horses were showing strain. Their breaths came harder, their sides heaving from taking great gulps of air.

Samuel and Hawk, as well as Lou, had had their life depend on these great beasts many times and had no doubt they would get them home one more time. They slowed as they saw the lights, giving the horses a small break. Samuel looked around; everyone was accounted for. He gave the nod and, again, they kicked the great beasts into a gallop.

They arrived in town just as the horses were about done in. The men dropped the girls and Jarod off at Autumn and Jarod's home.

"Check on Willow, will you, Jarod? I will see to your horse," Lou asked.

"Of course."

The rest of the men took the horses to the stable where it was warmer. They made quick work of taking off the saddles and took their time brushing them down. There was no doubt these horses had saved their lives again. Lou offered each of them a partial bale of hay and some oats, while Hawk filled the water troughs they had built inside. When the men had made sure their mounts were babied and taken care of, they left the stable.

Hawk went to let Gabe know they had made it back, and then after he warmed up, he walked down the street to Jarod's.

Lou went, first, to the house and lit the fireplaces in the living room and the bedroom before he walked to Jarod's.

Wynter and Autumn were busy warming and filling bowls of steaming stew. Autumn had gotten the telegram the boys had sent telling her they would be trying to beat the storm home. Wynter filled the men's cups with steaming coffee and the girls' cups with hot chocolate.

Autumn ran to Jarod, hugging him as she wept. "I was so

worried about you. The harder it snowed, the more worried I became. I am so glad you are all home safe."

After a hot, late meal, Samuel began leading Suzy out the door and down to the hotel. Hawk soon followed with Little Bird.

Jarod took Willow's hand and led her to the spare room to give her a look and to make sure she had not done anything to hurt herself or the baby.

Willow wanted to argue, but Jarod gave her that same look she had gotten from Lou, which meant she didn't need to even bother.

Lou watched, holding his coffee, as Jarod took Willow into the other room.

When Jarod came out, he had a smile on his face. "Nothing wrong with this girl a good night's sleep won't cure. She is, for sure, pregnant."

Lou stood as he took his wife's hand. "We will see you in the morning."

He walked Willow home and helped her put on her nightgown, then tucked her into a warm bed before he locked the doors.

"We will get Major tomorrow," he stated to no one, because Willow was snuggled into the blankets sound asleep.

Lou chuckled as he undressed and slid in next to her, pulling her into his arms.

The next morning, Willow was awakened by a cold nose burrowing under the blanket she had drawn over her head. When she lowered the blanket, she was greeted with a wet kiss. Major was licking her face excitedly, wagging his tail so hard, his entire body was moving. He stepped back to bark at her. All the while, Lou leaned against the doorway, his legs and arms crossed and a huge smile on his face. Willow heard the rumble of his chuckle. She threw both arms around Major and gave him a hug and kiss on his furry head. Rubbing his ears, she whispered in his ears, "I missed you, my old friend."

Lou stood holding out his hand in invitation. "Gabe brought him over; he has been fed. Come, little wife, Autumn has brought us breakfast. She said she had orders from Jarod to tell you no work today. He is also taking the day off. Everyone is invited to meet at Kayla's tonight for a family dinner."

"That was so nice of Autumn. I would have gotten up and made breakfast, Lou," she exclaimed.

Lou just shook his head. "You know Autumn. She is always looking out for her family. She did say not to get too used to it." As soon as Lou saw the hint of sadness enter her eyes, he pulled her into his embrace.

"She was teasing you, Willow. I can tell that old wives' tale of woman becoming emotional when they are pregnant is true."

Tears began to fill Willow's eyes. "I just feel like I am so loved here and finally back home where I belong."

Lou led her to her chair at the table, pulling her down into his lap. "Ah, little Willow, you *are* home, and home is where you will stay. I will never send you away again. I promise you."

She nodded her head and gave him a watery smile. "You have never broken your word. I trust you."

He gave her a hug as he stood, seating her and filling her plate before he filled his own.

"I am going to the office, but I want you to remember the rules. Always keep Major with you, no matter where you go, and lock the doors after me. Do you want me to send Missy over for a spell? Are you up to company? You had a hard journey."

Willow squirmed in excitement as she put another piece of bacon into her mouth. "Yes, please."

"No overdoing it, Willow. I mean it. You had a hard week. You may need more rest for a day or two."

"I want to talk to Missy about the baby. I want to know if she is due the same time as I am."

Lou shook his head and chuckled. "I can see Suzy and little Bird can't keep a secret."

"But, Lou, we have so much baby talk to discuss, and don't forget we have crocheting to do for Christmas."

Lou suddenly looked up in surprise. "Oh my Lord, Willow, with all this going on, I forgot Christmas is a month away." He stood quickly. "I have to discuss this with the men. I will be home in plenty of time for supper. Please, will you have a hot bath ready for me?"

Willow smiled. "Yes, Lou, I will have everything ready for you, but before you go, I want to clarify the rules, so I don't accidently break them. I am allowed out alone, as long as I have Major, is that correct? I can go to the mercantile or to Summer's, as long as I have Major with me? I would like to visit Roger's gravesite. I didn't get much time to say good bye to him."

Lou nodded his head. "Until I tell you otherwise, you are allowed to go where you please, as long as you take Major. Ben said he is ready to take over as your protector. Just as Starla is ready to protect Missy. Although Gabe told me Major snuck in with Starla, so they, too, may become parents." He wiggled his eyebrows.

Willow clapped her hands in excitement. "Oh, Lou, little puppies. I would love that."

Lou gave her a kiss before turning to the door. "I will ask Missy if she is willing to come for a visit. Behave, wife, and I will take you to the cemetery, tomorrow." He waited outside the door to make sure she locked it after him before he walked to the office.

Willow made quick work of straightening the kitchen while she waited for Missy. She gathered her yarn and needles. Looking for a snack for later, she found that she would have to make a cake or pie. She would wait until Missy arrived and ask her opinion, although she was pretty sure she knew her choice would be pie. She began gathering the apples from the pantry.

As soon as Missy arrived, the two girls began talking like Willow was never away. Willow told her everything about her visit to Boston, and Missy told Willow all about the events in town. Of course, the subject of babies came up, too.

"Those Wyatt boys have been coming to town more often, for some reason, and they have some new hands. Gabe said they are all no goods looking for trouble. They are not allowed at the Crooked Antler anymore. Now they go to the other side of town and cause trouble, but you know when there is a bunch of them, the sheriff always calls on Lou and Gabe to help. I think this town needs more deputies. I have mentioned it to Storm. Why should our men get called to help?"

"Has anyone talked to ole man Wyatt?"

"Yeah, but his sons will never do anything wrong in his book. He hires the lowest of the lowest. His boys get tangled up with them."

"Oh, well, I will mention it tonight at our family dinner. You can help make the argument to Storm. Maybe Samuel can bring it up to the governor. What do you want for a snack? Do you want to help me make an apple pie?"

"You know apple pie is Gabe's favorite. Let's make two, and I will take one home."

Willow knew that meant she would make two, and she also knew Gabe would think Missy made it. She didn't mind that her friend took credit for her baking. She did suggest several times that she let Suzy instruct her, so she could learn to bake her own. Missy never was enthusiastic.

Missy sat as they chatted, and Willow peeled and chopped the apples. She did get Missy to take the peels outside to where the compost pile was.

The girls spent a lovely afternoon going over what they still needed for the babies and what they were going to do for Christmas. Missy had confided in Willow that Little Bird had taught her to make some beautiful baskets. She had been saving the materials most of the summer. This really surprised Willow, who thought she knew all her friend was up to. Willow told Missy she didn't know what she was going to do yet. She avoided telling her friend she was almost finished making quilts for every family. She wanted to have enough time to make her baby and Missy one, also. Soon, it was time for Missy to leave for home with her pie, and Willow smiled as she waved goodbye to her friend.

As soon as Missy was gone, Willow hurried to prepare her bath first and lay out their clothes for the family supper. She was excited to spend time with everyone, except for Brenden and Shaun, of course. It would be very hard riding after all the snow.

At dinner, several things were discussed. Willow brought up not having enough deputies, and with Missy's help, they convinced Samuel to telegraph the governor and see about rounding up a couple more men. It was also decided that the men meet at the shop whenever they had time to work on different projects for Christmas. The women decided to all gather at Autumn's home to work on projects whenever they had time because Autumn didn't like to leave Wynter without help for the babies. Everyone was happy to see Willow, and they made sure to let her know she was missed.

Lou was watching Willow carefully, and as soon as the first yawn came out, he decided she'd had enough excitement. She took her by the hand and after bidding everyone goodbye for the day took his pregnant little wife home. He noticed Gabe and Missy were not far behind.

MISSING PAPA

Two weeks had gone by before Willow started having feelings like something was missing in her life. She could not put her finger on it, but she knew something wasn't right. Their sex life was fantastic and her life at the clinic was good. She was excited to hear about the nursery wing at the hospital. Lou had not argued with her or scolded her for anything. He either came home right from work or he let her know if he would be home late as the boys were all working in secret making Christmas presents in Samuel and Hawk's workshop. All the girls had been told in no uncertain terms they would be in big trouble if they dared to enter the shop. The girls were all busy with their Christmas projects. But something just wasn't right in Willow's world.

She had talked to Missy about it, but Missy didn't have a clue what Willow was talking about.

"I feel the need to do something naughty, like sneak a peek in Samuel's workshop."

Missy looked at her friend like she was a crazy woman. "Samuel will take a strap to you again. *No!* I will not be a part of that. Nope."

"I know, but since I have come home, Lou has let me do pretty much anything I want to. I am not used to this." Suddenly, her eyes got as round as saucers. "That's it! I am missing my papa. Missy, Lou has not given me any boundaries since I have gotten home. I hate to say this, but I need my papa, and I am going to do something naughty until Lou notices. He is not paying me the kind of attention I have become accustomed to. He used to know where I went and what I was doing. Now, it's like he doesn't care anymore. I feel like he doesn't love me enough to care." Willow sighed. "Maybe he doesn't care, maybe he only wanted me back because of the baby."

Missy shook her head. "Willow, if you would have seen what a mess he was when you were gone, you wouldn't say that."

"Then why doesn't he care what I do or where I go?"

"He is probably afraid you will leave again."

"I need him to take care of me."

Missy tapped her lips with her finger. This was her forte, causing mischief. "I think you should burn his breakfast or do something to earn a spanking."

"Yes, I can't tell him; he has to do this on his own."

"All right, give him a terrible breakfast and see what happens. I will come tomorrow, early afternoon, and if it works, great. If not, we will have to think of something else, but, Willow, don't blame me if you get a hard spanking. You are asking for it, after all."

Willow smiled, getting into the mood to do some major mischief. She would make Lou take her in hand, and then she would feel loved again.

The next morning, Willow put her plan into action. Lou got up with a smile on his face until he saw his breakfast. He looked in confusion, first, at Willow, who smiled at him, and then at the plate on the table. His bacon was burnt and his eggs rock hard. His toast was black and his coffee was so weak, it was like colored water. He cautiously looked at Willow and asked, "Is something wrong, darlin'?"

"No, Lou, everything is just fine. Why, is there a problem? I just overslept and got in a hurry." She tapped her foot on the floor, her arms crossed. "Don't you like your breakfast, Lou? I worked hard to make it just for you."

Lou looked up at his wife and her defensive stance. "I like it fine, wife." He smiled. "I am the one who kept you awake last night, so it is my fault you got up late. I am sorry, darlin'." With that, he stood to walk to the door and put on his coat and hat. "I will see you at supper, sweetheart." Giving her a peck on the cheek, he walked out and to the office. Gabe would share his breakfast and coffee.

When Lou explained what had happened as Missy poured him some coffee and handed him a plate of delicious fluffy scrambled eggs and sausage, Gabe shook his head. "I don't know what has gotten into her, Lou. Sounds strange. Don't you think so, Missy?"

Missy just smiled weakly. Obviously, a bad breakfast wasn't naughty enough. As she continued cleaning the kitchen, Missy thought about what they could try next. It had to be something dramatic to shake Lou out of his stupor.

On her way to Willow's home, she noticed the traveling salesman was in town again and she got a brilliant idea. She knew Lou had forbidden Willow to go near the tinker man. They usually were wanted men. As she entered Willow's cozy kitchen, she saw that her friend was making Lou and Gabe's favorite apple pie. Willow made one of the best as she had learned from Suzy.

"Instead of making one, why don't you make two? I will take one home to Gabe. It will be my reward for coming up with a brilliant new idea."

Willow turned to her friend. "I will make two if your idea gets me what I want. So, spill it."

Missy smiled as she took the coffee cup Willow handed her. She waited for Willow to sit with her own coffee before she laid it out. "You know the traveling salesman is in town today again. I thought Lou scared him out of town for good?"

Willow looked at Missy. "It may be a different man."

"Well, suppose Lou thinks you disobeyed him? Put yourself in danger again?"

It finally dawned on Willow just what Missy was saying. "You think I should go and buy something from the tinker man?"

Missy vehemently shook her head no. "Do not put yourself in danger for real. Just make it look like you bought something from him. I have a new bottle of whiskey; we can put some vinegar in it. You can serve it to him tonight. I'll put a bug in his ear about seeing you around the wagon."

Willow nodded her head eagerly. "That is such a good idea. You go and get the whiskey and bring it back, and I'll make our apple pies."

Missy entered their home carefully and went in search of the bottles she knew Gabe kept. They offered important clients a drink from time to time. She found three bottles in the cupboard in the men's office. Taking one, she snuck out to walk back to Willow's.

"Come, Starla, we must hurry back." When she arrived, she took out the bottle from under her coat. Setting it on the table, she opened the cork and poured a small amount into the back yard. When she returned, she handed the bottle to Willow, who put a small amount of vinegar in the whiskey bottle. Carefully, Missy put the cork back in and Willow stored the bottle in the cupboard.

Willow handed Missy the apple pie. "Now hurry home, and don't forget to put a bug in Lou's ear."

Missy agreed and, with a smile, left with her apple pie, which she would tell her husband she made. She stopped in midstride for a second. She wondered why her husband didn't care enough about her to notice she hadn't made the pie. Didn't he notice the home never smelled of apple pie fresh out of the oven? He didn't even know she couldn't bake. Willow would give her baked goods and she claimed them as her own and Gabe never noticed. She shook her head as she started walking again. She didn't want Gabe to notice. She hadn't had a spanking in a good long while and she wanted to keep it that way.

On her way home, she smiled and waved to Hawk as she passed him leaving the shop. Hawk shook his head as he waved. He was headed to the mercantile to see if the etched glass they ordered had arrived. Missy put the pie on the table and walked down to stick her head in the office. She had brought the men a fresh cup of coffee. She nonchalantly mentioned she saw the traveling salesman to Lou and Gabe. She noticed Lou paying particular attention when she mentioned seeing Willow out and about near the wagon. She excused herself to finish supper.

Missy hummed as she began their supper. She knew she was starting to lose respect for Gabe because she was fooling him so often and he didn't notice, but to her way of thinking, it was better than getting a spanking.

In the meantime, Willow had made a nice supper to make up for the miserable breakfast she had fed her husband. She had taken down some of the sausages she had bought and made potatoes and green beans. Everything was perfect when Lou finally returned home. She smiled sweetly as she dished up his supper.

Lou watched her carefully as she sat, and they began their meal.

"Missy mentioned she saw you in town today," Lou began. He didn't want to accuse her of wrongdoing if she was, in fact, innocent.

Willow smiled at her husband. She knew he was on a fishing expedition.

"Yes, I needed a few things at the mercantile. I was almost out of yarn. I did take Major with me, Lou. You did say it was fine with you."

Lou nodded, satisfied that she was telling the truth, but a nagging feeling in the back of his mind was bothering him. The way she didn't look him in the eye when she gave him her explanation. Everything was fine until supper was finished and Willow finished cleaning up. Lou was cleaning and oiling his rifle at the table when Willow opened the cupboard and got down the whiskey bottle. She poured Lou a generous drink and then a small sip for herself.

"I want to make a toast to my being home for a month and not having an argument the entire time."

Lou looked at her suspiciously as she lifted her drink. Willow rarely drank any spirits.

Her smile convinced him it was all right. Maybe she had gotten into the habit of an occasional drink while she was in Boston. He took a good-sized gulp, when it suddenly hit him that something was terribly wrong. He spit the amber liquid out and jumped up.

"What in the hell, Willow? What is this with the whiskey? Where did you get it?" And then the thought hit him.

"Willow, did you lie to me? Did you go to the tinker man when I had told you never to do it again?"

Willow looked down at her hands. If she looked him in the eye, she knew he would know she was lying.

"Yes, Lou, I did. I just wanted a bottle of nice whiskey to celebrate tonight."

Lou looked frustrated and confused. What had gotten into Willow and why was she acting like this? He needed to cool off and talk to some smarter men. He grabbed his hat and coat.

"I will come back when I cool down. I suggest you wait for me to return so we can discuss this." He slammed the door as he left.

Willow sat in the chair and thought about what she had done. She had lied to her husband to get a spanking. What was she thinking and why did she think this was a good idea? Why didn't she just talk to him?

Lou stormed into the shop. The men were all working hard on their respective Christmas presents. Lou and Gabe were making cradles and dressers while Samuel and Hawk were making beautiful jewelry boxes.

Samuel and Hawk looked up from their work as Lou stormed in and began pacing back and forth.

"What is up with you, Lou? What has got you so upset, as if I didn't know?" Samuel asked him innocently.

"It is Willow. She is acting funny lately. Naughty! I can't understand it. We have been doing so good since she is back, but suddenly, she is doing everything she can to earn a spanking."

Samuel smiled. "Have you been neglecting your duties as head of the household or Papa? She sounds like she is testing you to see if you still love her enough to protect her and guide her, correct her behavior. I had the same problems with Suzy one time, and that was the cause. Never did it again. I watched her like a hawk after that."

Hawk laughed. "And you can bet that little wife of yours is behind a good bit of it," he told Gabe.

Gabe looked confused. "What do you mean, Hawk? Missy has been very good lately. I haven't had to discipline her in months."

"I saw her walking home with another apple pie." Hawk explained, "Every time she comes home with baked goods that Willow made, she has caused some kind of problem. Willow pays her for her help in baked goods and you think she made them. Haven't you noticed your home doesn't smell of baked goods when you come home? Suzy mentioned one time, long ago, that Missy didn't know how to bake. She wasn't interested in learning. Have you ever seen a rolling pin or a spec of flour in your home? She can cook, but she can't bake. I have noticed that every time she comes home with baked goods, she has had her cute little nose in someone's business."

Gabe looked shocked by the statement. "I haven't, er, noticed her baking, but there is apple pie or cookies or cake at my table, so is it so bad to assume your wife made it?"

Hawk and Samuel both laughed out loud, before Samuel explained things for him, "As long as she is not causing problems, no one cares where your baked goods come from, but your little one is a troublemaker, always stirring something up. I will bet she had something to do with Willow's behavior, and I will also bet Willow needs her papa to show her she is loved. Now, I have Christmas presents to make, so you two take care of your women and leave Hawk and me to take care of ours."

Lou sat and thought for a minute before he stood up to leave and said, "Willow and I need to talk, and, Gabe, if Missy had anything to do with this, I expect you to take care of it." Having said that, he walked home, deep in thought.

Gabe excused himself, citing a need to have a chat with Missy.

When Lou arrived, he found Willow sitting in front of the fire crocheting. She looked up nervously as Lou walked over to her.

"Willow, we need to talk." He pulled her up and took her yarn, putting it on the coffee table before he pulled her onto his lap. " I want you to tell me the truth. Did you or did you not go to the traveling salesman today?"

Willow looked up at her husband, her fingers worrying themselves in her lap. "No, sir. I just, umm, felt like you didn't care about me because you haven't acted like my papa for a while." She looked down at her fingers before looking up at him again with tears running down her face. "I thought you didn't love me anymore," she wailed into his chest.

To say Lou was shocked was an understatement. Here, he had thought he was doing good. "Willow, if you truly felt this way, why didn't you talk to me? How can I fix it if I don't know it's broken? You have done me a great disservice."

"I don't know why. I was embarrassed to ask for my papa back. I thought you should know I needed my papa without me telling you. I am really sorry, Lou. I spoilt your breakfast on purpose and put vinegar in your whiskey."

"Where did you get the whiskey, Willow?"

Willow looked momentarily taken back. She didn't want to tell on her friend, but she didn't want to lie to Lou anymore, either.

"I don't want to tell you where I got it, but it was not from the traveling salesman," she explained, hoping it was enough.

Her hopes were dashed. Lou was not about to let her evade his question. "Do you get it from Missy?"

Willow miserably nodded her head, knowing she had just gotten her friend in trouble.

Lou continued to rock his wife while he took a minute to think this through.

"I am going to talk to Gabe. While I am gone, I want you to undress and stand in your corner. I want you to think about what you have done these last couple of days. I'll be back shortly to tell you what your punishment will be. Now go and do as I tell you."

Willow nodded and stood to go to their room, saying, "Lou, I am sorry I didn't just talk to you."

Lou nodded his head as he grabbed his hat and coat. "I am, too, little one. It would have saved everyone a lot of suffering. I will return soon."

He walked out the door and met Gabe just leaving the workshop. After a few words explaining what had happened, Gabe nodded his head. "I was just on the way home to confront Missy. Thanks for explaining things to me. I'll see you in the morning."

Lou started slowly back home, thinking as he walked. Willow had lied to him several times and had not told him something important to their relationship. She deserved to be punished, but she was also pregnant. He couldn't let this go, but he had to be clever.

He let Major out and back in again and made sure his food and water dish were full before he walked into the bedroom. He found his wife just where he told her to be. Naked and in her corner sniffling.

"Come here, Willow. Come and sit on my lap so we can discuss this—Papa to naughty girl."

Willow slowly walked to where Lou sat on the bed. He held out his arms for her and she came to him, sitting on his lap, burrowing into his chest.

"Now, as I see it, we have several things to discuss. The most important is that you kept information from me that I needed. The second thing is lying. You know that is unacceptable. Tell me, Willow, why is lying so bad?"

Willow mumbled, "Because it hurts our trust in our marriage."

"I want you to tell me again, and this time, look at me and speak clearly so I know you understand."

Willow looked up at him. "Because it hurts the trust in our marriage."

"What does not saying anything to me when something is bothering you do? Especially when it is something that concerns our marriage?"

"It is the same as lying. It hurts our marriage."

"Especially when I screwed up and we are just getting on solid footing again, correct?"

"Yes, sir."

"All right, here is what I am thinking. I want to make this lesson stick. But you are pregnant, and although I have asked Jarod and he told me I would not hurt the baby if I spanked you, I am not sure I feel comfortable spanking you hard. I want you to tell me how long you felt like you needed me and you didn't tell me."

"I didn't know what the problem was until yesterday. I knew I needed something, or something was wrong for a couple days before that, but I realized what it was yesterday. So, two days."

"All right, I am going to give you ten spanks with the paddle today and tomorrow for lying to me about the whiskey, and I am not going to let you come for two days, although I guarantee you will want to very badly.

Willow looked at him in horror. "But, Lou, two days. I cannot bear it."

"You can, and you will. Now, let us get the paddling over and get on to the good stuff. My good stuff and not yours."

Willow stood up as Lou reached over for her pillow. "Go and get me your brush, young lady, and then back over my lap."

Willow hurried to do his bidding, knowing from experience that the longer she took, the harder the spanking. She wondered as her hand wrapped around the large headed brush what she was thinking when she thought she wanted a spanking and a papa. She had to be crazy. She returned to Lou, who gently took the brush and laid it on the bed as he helped her across his knee. He made sure the top part of her body lay on the bed to protect her tummy. He handed her the pillow to hold on to.

He didn't wait long before the first spank started a burn that soon turned into a fire. By the tenth spank, her bottom was fully engulfed in flames. He turned her and held her on his lap, being careful to separate his legs so her bottom didn't sit on his rough denim. Her sobs tore his heart, but he knew he had to make this memorable. When she finally calmed, he put her back on the bed, looking at her as he undressed. This was going to be the hardest part for her. He didn't like making her suffer like this, but it was necessary.

He crawled over top of her and began kissing her neck and working his way down. He began sucking on first one breast and then the other, his teeth gently scraping as he nipped at her nipples. He could feel her hunger as he coaxed a response. She was fighting him because she knew what was coming, or *not* coming. His hand wandered down to her sexy little mound, searching until it found her swollen bud. His finger dove inside of her, gathering her juices as he lubricated her little button. Her breath hitched, and her bottom left the bed as she moaned with her arousal. He was igniting a different kind of fire, one that he would not allow her to put out until tomorrow night. He continued to circle her hot little bud, while she writhed beneath him, her breath coming in little pants, her body begging for his. She was truly breathtaking. Her breasts were becoming larger for the baby and the small baby bump only added to her beauty. He again drew her breast into his mouth, sucking harder, twisting the other until it was the twin's turn. He inserted two fingers into her silky, scorching hot pussy. He felt her clenching his fingers. She lifted her lashes, looking into his eyes with her own lust filled eyes, silently begging him to let her come apart. His gaze moved over her face as her breathing became ragged. He kissed her lips in a searing kiss. She was so close, he could feel the tension building in her, and then he stopped.

He looked down her as she began to beg.

"Please, Lou, don't leave me like this. It is cruel."

"Was it not cruel to play tricks on me and not tell me when something was bothering you? To leave me to try and figure out what was wrong on my own?"

He waited until she had backed off from the precipice slightly before he lifted her up on her hands and knees at the edge of the bed. Her juices were running down the inside of her thighs. He put his rock-hard cock to her entrance and impaled her, pumping hard until he felt his own climax coming. He came with a roar but stopped when he felt her on the edge of the precipice again. She would not feel her own pleasure until tomorrow.

Willow cried as Lou went to fill the basin with water to clean them. Her hand fell to her nub. Just a few strokes and she would have it. Just as she was about to take matters into her own hands, her husband returned. He put the basin down and walked over to her, pulling her hands out on top of the blanket.

"None of that." He rummaged into his secret drawer again and came up with two soft cuffs made of the softest leather. He came back and cuffed both her hands to the headboard before he cleaned them both. He crawled into bed and fell fast asleep while Willow didn't sleep a wink most of the night. Lou had woken up twice in the night and continued her lesson. This time, with her hands cuffed to the headboard. Each time, he had left her unsatisfied and wanting. She had just fallen asleep near dawn.

Lou finally woke after dawn and took the cuffs off before he let Major out for his morning constitutional. He began making breakfast. He could hear Willow softly sobbing as he walked in with breakfast on a tray.

"Eat up, sunshine. I will walk you to the clinic and pick you up. That is the only way I can be sure you are not negating your punishment. Tonight, I will give you what you need. Just like a good papa will always give you just what you need. I will warn you, though, I will know if you take care of yourself, and your punishment will be double."

Meanwhile, at Gabe and Missy's home...

As soon as Missy saw the thunderous look on Gabe's face, she knew she had been found out. Her hands shook as she finished setting the table, the apple pie in the center.

Gabe turned off the stove and then took her by the hand and sat her at the table, pointing to the apple pie.

"Who made the pie, Missy? And don't lie to me."

Missy nibbled on her bottom lip. "Willow made it; why do you ask?"

"You have let me believe, all this time, that you had baked them. Why did you lie to me? Why would you take advantage of someone you call a friend? Why not give her the credit she is due?"

"I never told you I baked the pies or cakes or cookies, Gabe."

Gabe looked up to the heavens, as if asking for patience, before he pointed to their room.

"Take off your clothes, Missy, and stand in the corner. When I return, we will discuss this and, Missy, do not test me any further. You are in enough trouble."

Missy quickly ran to their bedroom and began undressing until she remembered Ben was staying with them. Yes, his bedroom was at the end of the hall, but he could possibly still hear her punishment. Missy could hear the deep rumble of the men talking outside the door and just down the hall. She tiptoed to the door and put her ear to it. She could hear Gabe thanking Ben for giving them some privacy. Missy smiled. She knew Gabe would never humiliate her by punishing her in front of others. She quickly ran back to their room and finished undressing. She walked to her corner and began to think about why she was in trouble with her husband again. She had lied to him—not only about the baking; she had also coerced Willow into helping her with the crocheted blankets she volunteered for Christmas for the church. She fully planned on taking credit for all of them. Why did she take advantage of Willow? She was her friend, wasn't she? Since Gabe was onto her, he probably knew her part in their plot to fool Lou. She had stuck her oar in their marriage again, and that had gotten her spanked before. Missy began to twist her hands in worry. How did she get herself into these situations? It was all Willow's fault for being so weak. For not being able to figure her own way out of her problems. Why didn't she just tell Willow to talk to Lou? Missy smiled, even though she was looking at a good spanking again. It was so much fun trying to fool these men. She was good at it.

Gabe walked into the room with the paddle in his hands. Missy shuddered when she looked at it, quickly turning back to the corner. It was a good twelve inches long, with a handle on the end. Only two inches wide, it was made to sting and burn without leaving any bruising.

Gabe called her over to him as he sat on the bed. Standing her between his legs, he was so large, they were eye to eye, even though he was sitting on the edge of the bed.

"Have you thought about what you did the last couple of days? I want a list of it all, so we may take care of it all in this one spanking."

"I lied to you about the pies. I knew you thought I made the baked goods. Most of the time, I got them in receipt for ideas to get Willow out of trouble. I also volunteered to make crocheted blankets for the church for Christmas and planned on taking the credit for them, even though Willow made them."

Gabe's eyes opened wide in shock, but he quickly covered it up with a calm look.

Missy continued. "I came up with the idea to put the vinegar in Lou's whiskey, and I stole the bottle you had in the cupboard. I stuck my nose in their marriage again." She looked defiant as she added, "Some of it is your fault. I have thought about why I keep getting involved in their problems, and I have concluded that I am jealous of Willow. She has a papa who knows where she goes and what she does. He takes the time to correct her because he cares about her. The only time you pay attention to me is if someone tattles on me. By the way, you can thank Hawk or Samuel for tattling on me. I know they did it. They stuck their nose where it didn't belong, either." She pouted, her bottom lip sticking out so adorably. She stomped her foot in frustration before she finished, "You, on the other hand, don't even notice the kitchen never smells yummy like I baked. You never see a spec of flour or sugar. Have you ever seen a recipe book? You don't even know what I wore yesterday, do you? Even though I worked with you most of the day. Lou even sent her away to protect her. It was stupid of him, but he did it because he loved her."

Gabe looked in shock at his wife before he began thinking. What *did* she wear yesterday? Ah, yes, the pretty blue flowered dress.

"You are right, Missy. I don't pay you the attention you deserve. I will remedy that from now on, I assure you. You, on the other hand, have taken advantage of a friend, lied to me and meddled in her marriage." He sighed as he picked up the paddle. "I have punished you for those three things before. The punishment will, therefore, be the paddle and not my hand. You will remember this for a long while. I do not want to ever revisit these three things again. Do you understand?"

Missy looked at the paddle in his hand. She hated the thing. "Yes, sir, I will remember. I promise."

"Ten for each. That makes the total thirty. You will not enjoy this for the next couple of days. Then, tomorrow, you will go and apologize to Willow for taking advantage of her, and, Missy, you will tell the church women that Willow made some, if not most, of the blankets."

Missy grew panicky. "Gabe, you can't mean for me to tell those ole biddies that I lied? You know they look down on us already."

"You will not lie in church and especially not on Christmas."

"But, Gabe, they laugh at us already like we don't belong. They gossip about us at every opportunity."

"Then why did you volunteer, Missy?"

"Because I want to belong. Don't you see, Gabe? I act bad, so you treat me like the rest of the family treats the women—with respect and as the man of the family. They are loved and protected. Their men know where they are and what they are up to. They do the extra work to protect them."

"Are you saying I don't, Missy? Because, I assure you, I *do* know where you are, every minute." His startling blue eyes narrowed on his little wife. "You forget that I am an expert on human behavior. I know when to keep an eye on you. I just have to work and can't keep tabs on you every second. If you need attention, you need to tell me, so I can take care of the situation. In the meantime, I mean to remind you not to lie to me and not to meddle or take advantage of your friend. Over now; let's get this over with."

Missy went over Gabe's lap while he reached over for the pillow. "Hang on to the pillow, Missy, and do not put your hands back. I don't want to accidently hit them." The top part of her body lay on the bed.

"I am not going to give you as hard a spanking as you deserve because I am concerned about the baby. Jarod did tell me, within reason, it will not hurt the baby, but I would error on the side of caution. Ten of your spanks will be with my hand to warm you up before I use the paddle."

The first ten started to warm her bottom, the second began to build a fire, and the third ten set her bottom into a full-blown blaze. She was sobbing by the time he finished the warm up. She sobbed out her guilt at being such a poor friend, sobbed for lying to her husband, whom she knew loved her and tried to keep her safe. And she sobbed her misery at meddling in her friend's marriage and earning this spanking in the first place.

Gabe pulled her up onto his lap and rubbed her back as she cried into his shirt. He crooned to her words of forgiveness and love. When she had calmed down, he lifted her face to look at him, his angry blue eyes full of love now.

"I promise you, Missy. I will pay more attention to the things you do. I also promise you that I will hold you accountable when you need correcting, just like the rest of the family. I will stand by you when you tell the churchwomen you volunteered Willow's help. I will stand behind you when you apologize to Lou for interfering in his marriage again. I will leave it up to you to apologize to Willow, but I will ask Lou to make sure you did. Now, let us eat and have an early night. Ben will be gone to the widow Mellie's for a home cooked meal, and then he is off to the hotel for the night. We have the night all to ourselves. Let us enjoy it, shall we? Christmas is in one week, and I have much to do to get ready. I am depending on you to behave, so we can get our Christmas presents done."

Missy squealed in distress, "Oh, Gabe, I am not done with my gifts, either. I must spend time at Autumn's house with the girls to finish. We also have tons of things to do to decorate Kayla's for our Christmas supper."

Gabe smiled and replied, "Samuel and Hawk are going hunting for our turkey, day after tomorrow, and we all agreed to get together tomorrow, at dinner, and help you girls with the decorating." Gabe puffed out his chest and added, "Lou and I have volunteered to cut the tree, this year. Do you and Willow want to go with us on the sled? You can help us pick it out."

Missy clapped her hands in glee. "That would be wonderful. I can apologize to Lou while we go with you to get the tree. In the meantime, tomorrow, I must go to Autumn's house. Suzy and Little Bird are helping me with my projects."

It was settled as Missy began to warm their supper again. This time, they would enjoy the pie with no feelings of guilt.

"You know, little one, Suzy would also show you how to bake if you ask her."

"I know. When she asked last time, I turned her down and felt ashamed to ask later. I will ask her, tomorrow, if she will show me after Christmas."

Gabe smiled at his wife as she put steaming plates of venison and potatoes in front of him. "Good girl."

Missy smiled. It felt good to be called a good girl for a change, instead of troublemaker.

WILLOW FELT MISERABLE. She had finished her day at the clinic and it was expected that she and Lou go to Kayla's to begin decorating for their Christmas dinner. The next day, the boys were going to the forest to pick out and cut down their Christmas tree. The family was getting together for dinner and then to decorate, when all Willow wanted to do was cry. She was in so much need that just her legs rubbing together while she walked caused her need to grow. As soon as everyone was at the table for lunch, the conversation turned to decorating. The pretty glass bulbs that Suzy had carefully brought back from Boston sat at the next table—dozens of glass bulbs of all colors and shapes. They were all made in Germany and sent to the United States. Tin stars all ready to hang among the glass ornaments. The tree outside in back was situated right outside the large window. The girls would decorate it with nuts and berries and popcorn for the birds. The diners loved to watch the birds sitting on the branches having their lunch, also.

Anna Mae, Spring and Summer decorated the tree outside. Samuel and Hawk were helping the girls reach the top of the tree.

Gabe had talked to Lou about the girls going with them to hunt down the perfect tree.

"Willow, would you and Missy enjoy a ride to the forest to help us look for the perfect tree? We should be gone a couple hours at the most."

Willow nodded eagerly.

Gabe instructed them to hurry and put on their warmest hats and mittens and scarves. "Hurry, girls, no dilly dallying; we don't have all day."

The girls ran out the door with their dogs, hurrying down the street to gather their warmest clothes.

Lou and Gabe brought blankets for the sleigh to help keep the girls warm. Two sharp saws hung off the back in a compartment for tools. A large rope was put in, as well. By the time the girls returned all dressed warm and snug, the men were ready to begin. They helped the girls in the back seat while the men sat in front. Lou was handling the horses. Once they got to the forest, they tied the horses and began on foot. They had walked deeper into the forest for about a half hour when a projectile came flying and hit Lou and Gabe in the back. There was uproarious laughter from the girls. As they slowly turned, another snowball flew and hit each man in the chest. The men looked at one another, and giving a small nod, they took off running for the squealing girls, who knew by now they needed to run. Their short legs were no match for their men and they were soon caught. Lifting them both high in the air, the men stooped down and grabbed a handful of snow, rubbing it on top of the girls' heads. Their hats protected them, but it brought much laughter from the girls. By the time they had decided on the perfect tree and had it tied to the back of the sleigh, the girls' cheeks were rosy with cold. The men got out the blankets and wrapped themselves and the girls in them to keep warm. Lou and Willow sat in the front, and Gabe and Missy snuggled in the back. Lou and Willow heard laughter and squeals coming from the back occasionally. By the time they returned to the restaurant, the girls were frozen. The men sat them before a roaring fire while they untied the tree and set it up in the corner. The rest of the family began decorating the tree. Suzy and Little Bird handed out the bulbs and decorations, and the rest carefully hung them. Suzy handed each family a Christmas card to display proudly on the fireplace. Lou and Gabe brought the girls a steaming cup of hot chocolate as they sat and warmed themselves. It was the perfect time for Missy to talk to Willow.

"Willow, I want to apologize for getting you in trouble and for not giving you credit for all you do. I want you to know I am going to tell the church women you made most of the blankets, too."

Willow looked at her friend. "Missy, there is no need to apologize to me. I asked for your advice, and I knew you were taking credit for my things. You see, Missy, I was an orphan. I never had a friend before you. I just want to always be your friend. If it costs me an apple pie or a little crocheting, that is a cheap price to pay, in my book."

Missy looked at her friend with suspiciously shiny eyes before she gave her a huge hug. "You silly girl, you do not have to buy my friendship. It is freely given. Gabe is going to go with me to talk to the churchwomen when we go to Christmas service. I am going to tell them you did almost all of the blankets."

"I will go with you, too. I will let them know we are a team. You and me."

Missy wondered how she had gotten so lucky as to have a friend like Willow.

The men were standing quietly behind them, listening to every word. Lou nodded his head for Gabe to follow him. In the corner, Lou explained to Gabe about the churchwomen.

"Maurine is the pastor's wife. If she spent half her time looking for more people to help out and less gossiping about our girls, it would be helpful. She had Willow so in knots trying to keep up with everything they asked of her, I told Maurine to find someone else to donate. Our girls are not the only ones in this town. I think, when we go with the girls, we have another talk to the good minister about those old busy bodies.

Lou agreed, "Missy is amazing at numbers and organizing; as you know, she was a teacher until she became pregnant. She is not good at baking and crocheting. I think you are right. We will go with the girls and talk to the minister about them." It was agreed that they would take care of it without the girls knowing. Everyone made an early evening of it, after agreeing to meet at Autumn's in the morning.

Gabe took Missy home in the sleigh, so he could unhook the horses and put them away. On the way, he gave her a kiss. "I am proud of you, Missy. I heard you apologizing. You did very well."

Missy turned to Gabe. "Did you hear her say it was a small price to pay to be my friend? Gabe, I felt so bad for taking advantage of her."

"I think it will bring you closer and you will be true friends, like Lou and me. I am proud of you, and I have a surprise." He took out a large plate wrapped in a cloth. "I have supper for us. I had Kayla make us a plate, so you don't have to cook tonight, and we can stay by the fire and enjoy our night."

Missy reached up and gave her husband a kiss before she took the plate upstairs to their apartment and Gabe took care of the sleigh and horses.

Lou carried a similar plate wrapped in a large cloth with him as Willow and he walked home.

"I am looking forward to finishing your punishment, so I can give you some pleasure. I thought if all you had to do is warm up this plate of stew, we would have more time to ourselves." He wiggled his eyebrows.

Willow was more than happy with that arrangement. As soon as they returned home and Lou put some more wood on the fires and made the home toasty warm, he let Major out while Willow made sure he had food and water. She began to heat water for a hot bath before she went to her room and gently laid her nightgown on the side of the bed. She undressed, knowing she needed to get her ten swats over with, first.

Lou came in, filling the doorway and looking down at his little wife, who was no bigger than a spit. His little sprite. He had big plans for tonight. Punishment was over. He undressed and sat on the bed. "Come, wife, let us finish this and get on to the good things."

Willow agreed. She made quick work of putting the pillow where she could reach it and lying over Lou's lap.

Lou smiled; his little one had no idea what his plans were.

"Ten swats left; let us begin." The first swat stung and morphed into warmth as Lou gently rubbed the sting away. The warmth spread to her core, starting a fire that she would never be able to put out on her own, making her moan and squirm.

The next nine went the same as the first. Swat, sting, rub, until Lou pulled her close. Willow's breath was coming in pants now. He reached down, and just as he suspected, he found her soaking wet. He inserted first one finger and then two, pumping his fingers in and out until, with a yell, Willow came apart. He sat her on his lap with a smile on his face that reached his warm brown eyes.

Willow wrapped her arms around his neck and put her head on his shoulder. "Thank you, Lou. I needed that so badly." She could feel his arms tighten around her.

"No more secrets, little one. Promise me that if you are having any problems, you will come to me, so I can fix it. Promise!"

She eagerly nodded her head. "Why don't we have a nice hot bath, and then we can have some more fun before supper? Hmm?"

Lou agreed and helped her fill the tub. He'd had it made extra big like everything else in the house. He climbed in and waited while Willow followed him in front. They both leaned back with a satisfied moan. The water was perfect after their having been in the cold most of the day. Lou reached over and took the cloth he had laid there. Rubbing soap on it, he began to wash Willow's back. Massaging her tired muscles, he worked his way down. After he finished, she turned and straddled his waist, her head tipped back, her hair fanning the water.

Lou put a handful of shampoo in the palm of his hand after he wet her hair and began to massage it into her scalp, building a lather before he rinsed it. She lifted herself up and sat on his manhood, inserting it carefully inside herself as Lou began to lather her front. First, her breast got lathered as he pinched and rolled her slippery nipples, then, her stomach. He began to move his hips, pushing further inside of her as he rinsed her. He began to pump inside of her as he listened to her moans of pleasure, her head thrown back as he lifted her up and down on his shaft. He could feel her tighten inside before he began lifting her faster and harder on his shaft, deep moans escaping his own throat.

"Oh, Lou, oh, oh yes! Yes! Ahhhhh!" she yelled as she came apart and Lou was close behind her. He held her for a moment before he lifted her off and out.

"Why don't you dry off and put on the pretty see through nighty while I finish my bath and join you in front of the fire? I'll brush your gorgeous hair dry before you go to warm up our supper."

Willow hurried to do as he bid. She knew what nighty he wanted. The lemon yellow one she had gotten from Lori. It was so sheer that it was easy to see her body through it. She brought over the brush and laid it on the table before she sat in her chair before the fire. Lou had dried off and was just walking over when he heard a frantic knock on the door. Swearing, he tied the towel around his middle before he opened it. The deputy stood outside, shifting from foot to foot.

"I'm sorry, Lou, but the sheriff is gone, and I got a call from the Crooked Antler. One of the girls came running over saying a couple of the Wyatt boys were causing a ruckus. I need your help."

Lou swore in two different languages, at least. He knew, in his bedroom, his wife was brushing her own hair in a see-through nighty. Swearing some more, he walked in, grabbing his pants. He looked at his wife, who was smiling.

"I know, sweetheart, you have to go. Hurry back to me."

Lou walked over to give her a kiss before he buttoned his shirt. She could hear him cussing at the deputy, "You had better have gone to Gabe first, before you came here, or the sheriff is going to hear about it."

The poor deputy just kept saying he was so sorry and, yes, Gabe was waiting for him at the office.

Ada met them at the back door. The men could hear screams and breaking glass.

Ada just shook her head. "Shiloh is up there with Chet. He has one of his friends with him. Shiloh doesn't do two at a time. She tried to tell them that, but they are not listening." Another crash and scream got their attention. "Can you please get them the hell out of here? They were told by the sheriff not to come back. They wait until he leaves and then come sneaking back."

Lou and Gabe nodded and started up the stairs, only to hear more crashes and yelling. As they kicked in the door, Gabe had to duck as a glass just missed him to crash on the doorframe next to his head. That got his dander up and he drew his gun.

Lou yelled, " Stop!" shooting in the air with his gun. Everyone stopped. A slow, evil smile crossed both Gabe and Lou's faces as they looked at the two men. Lou could see the stranger inch his hands to the gun he had laid on the table before undressing to his long johns. His hand stopped moving as he looked into Lou's eyes. He could see his own death in the depths. Gabe's eyes were on Chet, cold and ready for anything.

Gabe waved his gun towards Lou, and when Lou had them both in his sights, Gabe looked at Shiloh and said, "Get out!" That was all he had to say to send her scurrying away.

"Now, boys, you are going to jail until the sheriff gets back. Chet, I would think your father would get tired of paying your bail. I would also think he would hire better men to work with you," Lou calmly explained what was going to happen. Gabe went behind them to put handcuffs on both men before he put his gun away.

"You gonna make us walk in the cold in front of the whole town to the jail in our long johns?" Chet whined.

Lou just laughed that humorless laugh he had. "Yep, you took me away from some good times with my wife. I am going to make sure you remember this for a while. The sheriff told you to stay the hell away from the Crooked Antler and Ada's girls."

"Come on; move it," the deputy finally piped up. That was when Lou and Gabe both decided to be in on the next hiring session.

Lou returned home to find his wife in her see-through nighty, her bottom swaying to and fro as she stirred the stew on the stove. She turned as he entered with a smile on her face.

"Yes." Lou thought he was a very lucky man. His cock got as hard as stone as she put his bowl in front of him with a hot cup of coffee. While they ate, he could see her dusky nipples through the material and the dark patch between her legs. The shadow of her slender legs when she turned to put the coffee pot back on the stove. God almighty, he could see the pink of her bottom and the dimple at the bottom of her back.

She turned back to him with a smile on her face as if she knew what she was doing to him, the little minx. She took her place and began to eat her soup slowly, licking her spoon, her little tongue coming out to savor every drop of soup. Lou kept looking at her as she ate, mesmerized as he watched her tongue licking the spoon. As soon as they finished, she began to pick up the dishes. Lou couldn't stand anymore. He got up to help her clean up, his cock pressing uncomfortably against the front of his pants.

As soon as all the dishes were in the sink, he lifted her in his arms and carried her to bed. She wrapped her arms around his neck and gave him a sizzling kiss as he lowered her to the floor. Quickly taking his clothes off, he began to undress her. Slowly, he lowered the straps as his hands shook. He looked at her beautiful breasts. Lifting his hands to them, he bent down to suck on one and then the other. Her skin was so soft, her scent clean and fresh. Her moan sent a wave of need straight to his cock. After undressing her, he lay her on the bed and just looked at the gift he had just unwrapped. He crawled into the bed and began to kiss first her neck and then worked his way down to her breast. He took one breast and then the other, working his way down to her pussy. He began his feast, lapping at her swollen nub, taking it in his mouth and gently sucking until her squirming became too much. She had caught his hair, and as her need grew more intense, she fisted it, arching her back and bringing her bottom off the bed as she twisted with a strangled moan. Her breathing became ragged as she dragged air into her lungs between moans. He ran his tongue over her slit and found her soaking wet. Lapping at her nectar, he felt her tight, silky folds quivering. Her sex clenched and dripped with hunger as he circled her hot engorged bud while he continued lapping. She cried out as she writhed under him, moaning with desire. Finally, he had mercy on her and inserted one finger and then two as he worked his way back up, drawing her breasts into his mouth one more time before he positioned himself between her legs. With one fluid motion, he impaled himself into her scorching hot sheath. He began pumping slowly, at first, but building momentum as he felt the tension building in her. Faster and harder until she cried out his name as she came apart with him following right behind her with a roar, his hot seed splashing inside of her. He quickly rolled off her, trying to catch his breath, his arms over his eyes as his ragged breath calmed. He rolled off the bed to the still hot water of their bath. Taking the washcloth, he cleaned himself before walking back to the bed and gently cleaning her. Putting the cloth back, he lifted her as he pulled the cover down and over her. He crawled in, pulling the blankets over them both and pulling her onto his chest into "her place" over his heart. He gave her a gentle kiss before closing his eyes.

CHRISTMAS

The next morning, he found his wife where he left her, curled up in his arms.

After he had kissed her eyes, she stretched before wincing. "Husband, I am a little sore and stiff."

Lou kissed her again before he got out of bed and put another log on the fire. He pulled on his long johns and walked out to let Major outside and to put another log on the fire in the living room, also. When he came back into the bedroom, he suggested, "How about we head to Kayla's for a good breakfast before you go to Autumn's? I'll be at the shop most of the day trying to finish my Christmas presents."

Willow sat up, pulling on her warm, flannel nightgown. She reached up to pull him down for a kiss, replying with a question, "What have you made for me, darling?"

Lou gave her a sweet kiss before he pulled on his boots and, giving her a swat on the behind to hurry her up, he gave her a wink. "Naughty girl, Santa will not bring you anything if you don't behave." He went back to let Major back in before he held out her coat and mittens and then handed her the scarf.

They headed to Kayla's and met Gabe and Missy heading the

same direction. When they entered, they found the rest of the family had the same idea. They all had a lovely breakfast before the men headed to the shop and the women all congregated at Autumn's house. The women worked all day on their projects. Little Bird and Missy hid in the big bedroom and worked in secret while the others worked on quilts and crocheting. Suzy was busy making moccasins with beautiful beadwork. Summer was finishing hers at her own home, and Anna Mae and Spring had left with Brenden and Shaun to finish up their gifts at home. They would all meet at church on Christmas day.

Meanwhile, the men were working hard finishing the sanding and putting on porcelain nobs and hinges. Mark had made a new dresser and a new rocking chair. Jarod, a new dresser for the babies and a new dresser for Autumn. Lou had made a new china cabinet with glass in the two front doors. The men had paid dearly for the delivery of the etched glass. Samuel had helped them with the carving of the claw feet on the bottom and the top. He was in the process of helping Gabe with a similar cabinet. Little brads held the glass in place, but it was delicate work. Both girls would get new china cabinets. Hawk and Samuel had their own secret plans as they worked on large jewelry boxes. They showed the boys how they worked—when they lifted the top lid, a little dancer came out, singing, in Samuel's case, *Oh, Suzanna* and, in Hawk's, *Birds in the Night*. The little dancer twirled around as the music played. When the lid was set down, the music stopped. Each box had two drawers in the front with two small etched glass doors to hide the drawers. They were beautiful, and Samuel and Hawk worked diligently for many days on them, sanding them until they were perfectly smooth and the drawers opened easily. The tiny hinges and brads took a great amount of care. The glass was special ordered to be the exact size, with beautiful birds etched into each door. The men were very proud of their work, but they had a secret no one else knew about.

The week flew by as everyone worked hard at finishing their projects. Soon, it was Christmas day. Everyone dressed for church first thing after breakfast. Samuel, Hawk and Lou got out the three sleighs and hooked them up. Between the three, the family could all ride together to church and take their seats near the front. They arrived a few minutes early to carry in the blankets the girls had made.

Samuel, Hawk, Jarod, Lou and Gabe went to find the minister in his office behind the podium. Missy and Willow accompanied them. Lou knocked firmly before entering. The minister, a fifty-something-year-old man, sat back in his chair as he looked at the men walking in. Lou and Gabe put the blankets down on the long table before Gabe said, "Reverend Springer, I would like a word with you if you have a second?"

The reverend stood, motioning to the chairs.

The men declined, saying, "No, thank you, Reverend, we have come to say our piece. You see, your wife and the others have been putting a hardship on our girls. They have asked them to contribute more than their fair share, simply because they are too lazy to find more volunteers."

The man looked confused. "You mean my wife and the other ladies of the guild? I assumed they were doing most of the crocheting." He looked over at the pile the men had deposited on the table. "I guess I was wrong." He walked over to the door and let out a shout that was heard clear at the back of the church, "Maurine, I want you and the rest of the guild to get your bottoms in here, and your husbands had better come, too."

It wasn't long, and the small office became crowded. The reverend said to his wife, "What, exactly, wife, is your contribution to the poor this year?"

Maurine looked at her normally meek husband. "Asa, you know very well, we recruit help to help us with the gifts for the poor at Christmas."

"Help, Maurine? I haven't seen where *you* helped at all. What about you, Clara, or you, Mable? What have you contributed?" The husbands began to get suspicious looks on their faces, like they knew something was wrong and they were not going to like it.

Lou spoke up before the women started making excuses. He pointed to Maurine. "Did I tell you last Christmas that you needed to find more help besides Willow?" He turned to the reverend then and added, "Willow spent weeks crocheting blankets last year. She was the only one who made them. Samuel and Hawk had already told your women not to ask their wives because of the same thing."

Martha spoke up before her husband got any ideas, as this was not looking good. "We asked Missy this year."

"Missy is not very good at crocheting." Gabe looked lovingly at his wife. "She is the best schoolteacher and bookkeeper and organizer this side of the Rockies, but she doesn't crochet well. She asked Willow to help, knowing that Willow would end up doing most of the work."

Maurine smiled a smug smile. "We knew she would ask Willow to help."

Reverend Springer's face began to turn red as he asked, "You asked Missy to help, knowing she would ask Willow? After Lou told you Willow would no longer carry the whole load? In the meantime, what have you women been doing?"

Samuel spoke up as he leaned over and looked Maurine right in the eye. "They go around town gossiping about these two girls, for one thing, and anyone else they can gossip about. That is why you cannot find any volunteers, isn't that right?" He straightened to his considerable height.

The husbands of the women began to talk amongst themselves angrily.

"Is this true, Martha?"

Martha began to shake her head no, but before she could begin, Hawk stepped in.

"I have heard them, myself, many times. In the mercantile, they stand gossiping like a bunch of old hens."

Martha's husband began tapping his foot, his arms folded in front of him, frowning at his wife.

He turned to the other husbands and declared, "Martha will not be going anywhere with the other women for a very long time. She has to prove to me she has repented. I expect to see either ten crocheted blankets or quilts before I even consider it. She will not have an easy time sitting to do it, either. Come, wife, our seats are waiting. You might enjoy sitting on a comfortable bottom while you can." He took his wife by the arm before he turned to Willow and Missy and said, "My apologies for my wife's doings. She will be by to apologize, herself, later. Gentleman." He tipped his hat on the way out.

The rest of the husbands did exactly the same. "The same goes for the rest of our wives. Do not worry, Reverend. Next year, they will have more blankets than you can shake a stick at. Each one will bring in ten blankets."

Finally, the only ones who were left were the reverend and his wife, Maurine. "You heard the men, Maurine. You are no better than they are. Ten blankets and, wife..." He hesitated for emphasis. "We will be having a serious discussion after lunch."

He turned to the men. "Thank you for bringing this to our attention. Rest assured, it will be taken care of."

They all filed out to find their seats. They could hear the good reverend scolding his wife through the heavy door. The congregation sat and waited for the sermon, but before the reverend started, he called his wife up to the podium.

Maurine cleared her throat before she looked out over the crowd. "It seems I have a heartfelt apology to give. I want to apologize to everyone I have hurt with my gossiping. My husband has shown me the error of my ways. I promise I will never gossip again." She looked over the crowd and added, "I owe Missy, Willow, Little Bird and Suzy a special thank you for making all the blankets for the orphanage the last couple of years. I am truly sorry you didn't have more help. I promise to recruit more help next year.

This year, the guild will provide all that will be needed. I will, however, be asking for help in the summer again." She stepped down with her head held high as she sat in the front pew to await her husband's sermon.

After church, the men dropped the women off at home and went to the shop. They would haul all the new furniture to the homes where they belonged while the women, with Brenden and Shaun's help, carried theirs to the tree at Kayla's. After everything was delivered, the family and a few close friends congregated at Kayla's. The help had done a wonderful job. Mouthwatering smells greeted everyone as they entered, and the tree was full of presents underneath.

As everyone was seated, Samuel gave a prayer of thanks before the food was passed around. Mounds of whipped potatoes and creamy gravy, chestnut dressing and turkey and goose, along with cranberries and every kind of vegetable imaginable was on the table. The empty table was full of pumpkin pies, apple pies, mincemeat, and of course, Samuel's favorite, cherry pie. The workers who had done the cooking sat and ate with everyone else. Kayla was careful to ask the ones who didn't have families to serve and clean up but, also, to spend Christmas with the rest of the family.

After everyone had eaten their fill and was rubbing their tummies or letting out their belts, Samuel and Hawk began giving out the children's toys. The little ones were all laughing and excitedly opening their gifts. The men had carved out horses, cows, wagons, and buggies while Samuel and Hawk made big barns out of scrap wood—big enough for all the equipment. The boys loved them.

Suzy and Little Bird had made new dollies and doll clothes for the girls. The men had crafted small cradles, tables and beds to fit into the dollhouses that Samuel and Hawk had made. The older kids got new ponies, which they had to wait until spring to pick up.

Then it was time for the husbands to see their gifts. Suzy and Little Bird had ordered the woodworking tools they had asked for.

Suzy had also made moccasins. Autumn and Willow made quilts for each home, and Little Bird and Missy made leather coats for each man, with fringes hanging from the arms.

The women loved their furniture, and each one received from their husbands a small jewelry box, with drawers and a little dancer that danced when the top was opened. Little Bird and Missy had also made beautiful baskets for everyone.

When they were finished opening their gifts, both Samuel and Hawk pulled out their chairs, inviting their wives to sit on their laps. Out from the kitchen came one of the waiters with a guitar, playing a love song and walking to the two couples. Behind him came two waiters with huge jewelry boxes—a foot high with a top that opened and a porcelain dancer that popped up. The front doors were made of beautiful etched glass doors with beautiful birds on each door. Inside were three drawers. The waiter placed a box in front of each woman, their eyes wide as they each squirmed in their husbands' laps. The guitar player stood before them until the love song was finished, and then he walked back to the kitchen.

Samuel started, "Suzy, when we got married, your folks didn't approve of me and we had to have a small, hurried wedding. I am telling you now, if you want a big fancy wedding, I am ready to marry you again in any church with however many people you want."

Suzy looked into Samuel's eyes, the eyes that had twinkled with humor or snapped with anger. She had loved him all these years.

"I don't need another wedding, Samuel. I have you and my family, and that is all I need to make me happy."

Samuel smiled as he opened the first drawer. Inside was a small box. He handed it to Suzy.

Her hands trembled as she opened it. Inside lay a beautiful ring, the stones all different colors. Five stones, one for each of the children.

"Each is their birthstone. Brenden, Spring, Summer, Autumn, and Shaun," he explained.

Tears glistened in her eyes as she burrowed into his chest, looking at the ring as he put it on her finger.

"I know our family is the most important thing in the world to you, so this ring signifies our life. Now, in this second drawer..." he opened it and took out a piece of paper "...is another present.

He opened it to show her. "This one is for both of you." It was a deed to a piece of property just outside of town.

"It's between Storm and Wynter's place and town. The boys have promised to build us a duplex. Half the building will be a home for Little Bird and Hawk, and the other half of the building will be our own separate home. We will both have our own home but be in the same building, about a half hour from town."

Suzy began to bounce up and down, clapping her hands until Samuel stopped her. "My little Suzy, if you don't stop with the wiggling, we won't get to the last part. This is for the both of you, as well." He opened the third drawer and drew out another piece of paper.

Hawk had opened the third drawer of the other box at the same time. They handed their wives the papers. *Tickets to Paris.*

This time, Hawk spoke, "Samuel has asked us to join them on a cruise to Paris for the summer. We leave in June, but we will be here to see these girls have their babies before we leave. By the time we get home in October, I am told by the boys that our home will be finished. Our daughters have promised to have it stocked with canned goods, and the boys have promised to have the wood hauled and meat butchered and in the cold shed."

Tears glistened in Little Bird's eyes, also, now. Hawk opened the second drawer of her box. Inside was another little box. This ring had all the grandchildren's birthstones.

Both girls wrapped their arms around their husbands' necks as they easily lifted them.

Turning to the others, Samuel bid them farewell, "We would like to thank you all for making this a Christmas to remember. Now we will take our wives home to be properly thanked." He winked as he turned to leave.

The rest of the family remained to drink hot cocoa and sing Christmas carols. It was a long night, but everyone helped with the cleanup, and before they knew it, all the children were home in bed, waiting for Santa to come to their home with more treats and toys.

Lou opened the door and put his hands over Willow's eyes as he took her into the house. She giggled as he led her to the living room and then took his hands away. Her gasp of delight warmed his heart.

"Oh, my Lord, Lou, it is beautiful. It must have taken you so long to make, and it must have cost you so much money."

"Gabe and I gave Samuel money to order us a real set of china. Good china, for when we have special company. We will be spending money on the baby, too, but I wanted you to have something nice just for you."

"Do you mean Missy got a china cabinet, too?"

"Yes, but while yours has birds etched into the glass, hers has flowers. We ordered different glass."

Willow reached up to pull Lou's lips down to hers. "Let me reward you properly," she said with a wink.

SPRING AND BABIES

It was finally spring. The tulips were poking their little heads out of the snow that was left and the air was warmer during the day. Willow could finally open the windows for a little while during the noon hour and let some blessed fresh air in. She was as big as a beached whale and waddled like a duck, but she knew her time was soon. She stood up to stretch, putting her hand on her back. Wynter had lent her some of her maternity dresses and they were very pretty, but Willow could not wait to get her figure back again. She smiled as she cleaned the waiting room. Soon, the workmen would start on the new hospital. When she had finished, she called Major and locked up. Walking home took a little longer these days, but by afternoon, it had warmed up some and the walk felt good after a long winter. Major stayed close by her side. It was still early afternoon, so she decided to lie down for just a few minutes before she decided what to have for supper. She was awakened by the featherlike kiss of her husband. He stood next to the bed smiling.

Willow jumped up, but Lou just pulled her into his arms as she struggled. "I need to start supper, Lou, please let me go."

Lou just laughed and said, "We decided to go to Kayla's for supper."

"Who is we, Lou? You know I don't feel like going out and having everyone look at me."

Samuel, Hawk, Jarod, Gabe, all of the wives and us. Just family, Willow."

Relief filled her eyes. "That sounds fine. I am interested in hearing how the packing is going for their trip."

Lou laughed and said, "I think Samuel just wants to have supper together because he wants to check things out and see how long before the babies come. He knows the girls won't want to go until you give birth, and the trip is only a month away."

Willow slapped Lou on the arm. "You are so silly. I think it will be in the next week. The baby has dropped. The same for Missy. Do you know we take up the whole boardwalk if we walk side by side?" She laughed at her own joke.

Lou took her coat off the peg and handed it to her. Taking her by the hand, he walked with her down the boardwalk the three blocks to Kayla's. Willow was all for not having to cook supper. Truth be told, she had not felt good all day. Her back was hurting.

Lou pulled out her chair for her before he took his own, as usual. Missy and Gabe were already there, as well as the rest of the family.

Missy was rubbing her back, too.

Willow asked, "Is your back hurting, too? I can't seem to make it stop."

Missy nodded. "My Lord, it has been bothering me all day. I can't seem to get comfortable."

Jarod looked up at the girls, paying close attention to what they were saying. He looked toward Samuel, who was also watching them closely. Samuel and Jarod both gave Gabe and Lou a sharp kick under the table while the rest of the women were chattering away. Samuel looked at Lou and Gabe and ever so slightly nodded his head towards their wives. The two expectant fathers began listening to the girls comparing their woes. They both looked back at Jarod and Samuel, who again smiled and nodded. Throughout dinner, they looked at their wives every so often to make sure they were still all right.

Willow was the first to feel a pinch about halfway through the meal. Suzy looked at her as she moaned softly, rubbing her tummy. She turned to look at Jarod to make sure he was paying attention and received a slight nod as well.

When Missy doubled over suddenly, Summer jumped up out of her chair and said, "You girls should both go to the clinic."

Willow and Missy looked at one another, confused, until it dawned on them what was happening.

"We are almost finished with our meal. Let us finish first," Willow thought out loud.

Jarod agreed it was early stages yet but told them it wasn't a good idea for them to eat any more food. Most everyone in the family was at the restaurant, which left no one to track down.

Lou and Gabe carried the girls out the door and to the clinic, gently setting them each on an examining table. Hawk had left slightly earlier to fetch Don and Jennifer. The boys stayed with their wives as they undressed and put on fresh clean gowns that opened in the back. As soon as Donald and Jennifer arrived, they were shagged out of the room, giving the girls privacy to be examined. Lou went to telegraph his brother, and Gabe left to let Ben know. When they returned, things had changed. The girls were in full-blown labor, both rooms filled with moans. The husbands began to pace. Samuel knew the routine after all the family births. He brought out a bottle Hawk had stopped to get—Samuel's finest whiskey, straight from Ireland and special ordered. He saved it for very special occasions such as these. He took all the men outside while the women sat patiently crocheting or reading or talking amongst themselves. Samuel passed the bottle around, handing it to Lou and then Gabe. He encouraged them to take another good drink.

"You're going to need it," was all he had to say. Lou and Gabe had sat in on these family births before. They knew what to expect, but watching others going through it and having their own wives go through it was completely different. The rest of the family tried to keep them outside talking with the rest of them as they continued to pass the bottle.

Lou continued going inside from time to time, but when he heard a moan from his side of the clinic, Samuel quickly took him back outside.

Willow tried not to cry out. She knew if she made too much noise, her husband would barge through the door, no matter how many men tried to keep him out. It was impossible towards the end. The labor was too intense and lasted far longer than it should have, in her opinion.

"Jarod, please hurry. I can't keep quiet much longer."

Jarod just chuckled. "You haven't been that quiet, little one. I am thinking Samuel is having his hands full keeping Lou and Gabe calm."

"Oh my God, Jarod, this is going to be a bad one; I can tell."

"Yell if you have to, Willow. Let them worry about your husbands. You have two centimeters to go yet. It could be quick or it might take a while; there is no knowing."

"Not hours, Jarod, pleeeese tell me not hours, Oh! *Oh!*"

"Not hours, little one. Soon, maybe a half hour or maybe in five minutes."

Willow rolled onto her side, clutching her stomach in abject misery.

"I will never go through this again. Never, never, never!"

Jarod put her feet into the stirrups again as he patted her arm. He went to the front to check how close she was. She was beginning to push with the pains.

"I can see you are ready to birth the baby now. Willow, hang on to the rails, and when you feel like pushing, push as hard as you can. It may take a couple of pushes, but you know that."

Willow nodded as the next contraction hit. A scream escaped as she pushed as hard as she could.

"It is coming. I can see the head. One more with the next contraction should do it."

No one had ever said sweeter words to her than 'the next one should do it'. She could hear a scuffle outside and knew the men were having problems. She heard Missy's scream, as well, and more scuffling. Finally, she heard Suzy's usually calm voice raised in anger. Willow smiled as she pictured it.

In the waiting room, after Willow's scream, it took all four of the men to hold Lou down, and then, when Missy screamed, they had to divide up. Hawk and Mark tried to stop Gabe while Samuel and Storm tried to hold Lou. It wasn't working so well. The men broke free, only to be confronted by the angry women, standing with their arms crossed and tapping their feet. Suzy stepped up to Lou and Little Bird to Gabe.

Lou looked down at the little woman who was poking him in the chest with her finger. "You. *Poke.* Will. *Poke.* Sit. *Poke.* Down." *Poke, poke.* Then came the finger shaking. "You boys know better than this. When the girls are cleaned up and ready, Jarod and Donald will come for you. *Now, sit!*"

Lou looked ashamed as he turned to go back to his chair.

"Yes, ma'am," was all he said. He sat next to Gabe and they waited some more. Both of them rubbed the front of their pants as their palms became sweaty. Beads of sweat covered their foreheads as the moaning continued, and then another scream sent both men to their feet.

Suzy pointed back to the chairs angrily, and both of them sat down again.

Lou turned to Gabe and said, "I would just as soon take a beating as this."

Gabe wholeheartedly agreed.

Just then, they heard a slap and the cry of a very angry baby. It was repeated, seconds later, in the other room. Both of the men looked at one another with huge shit-eating grins on their faces. The stood to wait patiently for their turn to enter the delivery room, their chests puffed out in pride. They had watched the other proud fathers down through the years enter the delivery room first —Storm, Brenden, and Shaun—but now it was their turn. As soon as the door cracked open to both delivery rooms, the men raced in.

Jarod said, "You have a healthy baby boy and the mother is doing very well." A sigh of deep relief left his lips before it was replaced with a smile. He walked over to Willow, who held a tiny pink baby. The baby was sucking on his mom's breast hungrily, making noises of contentment as he sucked. Willow had the most beautiful look on her face, one of love and happiness. She had a pillow to keep the baby in place next to her.

When she held out her hand to Lou, a team of horses could not have kept him away. He took it and placed a gentle kiss on her gorgeous lips. "I am so proud of you, Willow. Look what you have given me."

Willow smiled a tired smile as the baby finished with a tiny sigh and fell asleep in her arms. Jarod stepped in between them and gently took the baby to the crib near the foot of the bed. Covering it carefully, he turned to Lou. "Are you ready for the rest of the family? I prefer to have them all come in at once and get it over with, so Willow can get some rest all the sooner."

Lou agreed as he sat in the chair next to his wife, still holding her hand.

Jarod opened the door, and everyone but Gabe came in. Samuel, Mark, Hawk and Storm all stood to the side and allowed the women to see the baby first. The room was filled with, "Oohs and ahhhs and isn't he beautiful," as the men waited patiently. They had learned, long ago, it wasn't worth their lives to get between the women of the family and the baby until they had their fill.

Lou looked at Storm's cut lip and Samuel's red, soon to be black and blue, cheek. He turned to Willow with a smile. "After I leave, I have to clean up some collateral damage."

Willow tsked at her husband. He could see she was pretty much done in. As the ladies came to the bed, they could see it, too.

"We will let you sleep as soon as the men are finished seeing the baby. We are going to Gabe and Missy's room next. Missy had a boy, also, did you know?" Suzy imparted the news.

Willow's eyes filled with tired tears. "Oh, Lou, our son will have a playmate."

Everyone left as quickly as they had come. Lou stayed until Willow fell asleep.

Jarod patted Lou on the shoulder. "Congratulations, Daddy. Now, why don't you say your apologies and go home and get some sleep? Jennifer has volunteered to stay the night. She and Donald will sleep in the doctor's quarters tonight. That assures everyone that they are close. Willow will need you first thing in the morning."

Lou agreed, "I will see Gabe's little one, first." He walked in to see a very proud Gabe holding Missy's hand as she tiredly smiled. When they all had left the mothers to get as much sleep as the babies would allow, Lou apologized, along with Gabe, to all the family. They all smiled and said they understood, and the men went home, content and happy.

THE DREAM

It had been two months since the babies were born. Both Willow and Missy switched babysitting when they could, and Autumn and Summer stepped up when they couldn't. It was so nice to have family close. Hawk, Samuel, Little Bird and Suzy had left soon after the babies' births for their cruise. They stayed only long enough to see the children christened and the godparents named. Gabe and Missy were godparents to Johnathon, and Lou and Willow were godparents to Samuel. They had decided, long ago, the firstborn boy would have Samuel's first name and the second born would have his middle name. Samuel was so honored that he gave both baby boys a scholarship to the college of their choice.

Today was a beautiful late spring day. The days were getting longer and warmer and even the nights were warming up. The girls had all gotten the gardens planted while taking turns babysitting. They were meeting their husbands at Kayla's for supper as Autumn had agreed they needed a night to themselves. She knew how much this night meant to the girls. She knew Jarod had given the go ahead to begin their sex life again after the babies. Lou had ordered a bottle of Kayla's finest wine. Gabe was celebrating at home but had a bottle of the same wine. The girls had gone to Lori's as they wanted to pick out the prettiest and sheerest nighties Lori had.

Lori laughed at their request. "I ordered two of the prettiest, the day I heard you two were pregnant, yellow for you, Willow, and a light blue one for you, Missy. I have been waiting for you to come and ask for them." The older woman had a twinkle in her eye as she held them up, one at a time, for the girls to see.

Willow clapped her hands in glee. "That is so beautiful, Lori. Look, Missy, the tiny flowers all across the top barely hide my breasts. The rest is so transparent, down to here, where the flowers hide my, um, you know, and bottom. I love it, Lori, thank you so much."

Missy looked at her nightgown, blue with tiny birds that were placed in exactly the same place as Willow's flowers.

"Just enough to give the men a peek and whet their appetites. I love mine, too." Both girls gave Lori a huge hug before taking their purchases to the counter for her to ring them up.

Suddenly, there was a commotion on the street—guns firing, men shouting, horses galloping.

Lori looked out the window and yelled, "Looks like someone is robbing the bank!" She ran to lock the doors, but before she could finish, the door burst open and a young man in his late twenties came running in with wild eyes, waving a gun. Willow was closest to him. He grabbed her with his arm around her neck and his gun waving wildly at the other two.

"Get back. I don't mean to hurt her, but I will if you two don't let me go out the back way." Both women stepped aside as he dragged Willow clawing at his arm around her throat, trying to get him to loosen his hold.

"You don't know who you are messing with, mister. That is big Lou's wife you got there. He will kill you for sure. Let her go and run; you may have time to get away."

"Lou beat me and hauled me and my boss's boy to jail in our long johns. Walked us right through town. This is as good a way as any to get back at him." He jerked Willow up higher, leaving her feet kicking in the air. "Now, you two move against the wall." His smile was evil, his eyes glazed with fear and rage. The man walked to the back door just as Lou and Gabe ran in. Lou's eyes got wide as he saw his wife in the man's arms with a yellow nightgown held tight in one of her arms. She was caught between his arms and her hand, trying to pull his arm down. His dream came flooding back and a cold dread entered his eyes. Fear like he had never known slithered down his spine, almost bringing him to his knees. Gabe's voice brought him back to thinking this through again. He knew he had to use his head.

"Let her go, and we'll give you a head start. If you hurt her, you are a dead man," Gabe growled. The man continued dragging Willow out the back door and towards a horse.

Willow was seeing stars, gasping for breath and dragging her feet, trying to slow the man down. Finally, outside, the man stopped, pulling his gun up and next to Willow's head.

He smiled an evil smile as he looked at Lou and said, "Well, well, the big and bad Lou. I want to see you beg for your wife's life. Get on your knees and beg."

Lou threw down his gun, opening his arms wide, exposing his chest, his arms straight out to his sides. He knew if the man shot at him, Gabe would get him and Willow would be safe. He would sacrifice his life for Willow's in a heartbeat and without a second's hesitation.

"Why would I care about her? You have me mistaken for someone else." He kept walking towards the man and Willow, one slow step at a time. "Go ahead and shoot me if you think you can, but she means nothing to me." He took another step.

The man pointed his gun at Lou as Willow screamed, "No, Lou, no!" with what was left of her breath. She struggled mightily but the man had her tight. She heard the hammer cock, felt the darkness creeping up to claim her and the intense sadness. If Lou died, she did not want to live, either. Tears fell onto the man's hands as darkness began to take her. Just then, she heard the sweetest words in her entire life.

"Sic 'em!"

Missy had the dogs and had given the order to kill. The dogs ran toward the man. He panicked and lowered the gun to shoot the dogs, but it was too late. Major jumped on the man's back, knocking him down to his knees while Starla bit down on the wrist holding the gun, snapping bones. Willow fainted in a puddle on the ground. No one could get close enough to catch her. The dogs tore at the man. Major was in a rage and would not stop after repeated attempts by Missy. He had waited obediently for his command, but it took all the dog had. He was ready to jump without the command at any second.

The man's screams echoed in the distance in her mind as she began to come around. Lou ran to her and pulled her up, lifting her into his arms as he ran with her to the clinic, the pretty yellow gown left behind in the blood. Not Willow's blood, thank God. He ran to the clinic, kicking open the door and running for the first table he came to, yelling for Jarod. Gabe and Missy followed with the dogs. Major would not settle, whining at the door until Jarod opened it and let him in. The dog walked to Willow, licking her hand as Lou stood on her other side.

Willow opened her eyes and smiled at the dog. "Good boy," she said. Major barked and lay down near the door while Jarod made quick work of looking her over.

He smiled at a worried Lou as he reassured him, " She is dirty but fine. She may have a sore throat for a day or two, and I hate to say it, but you should probably postpone the plans you had for the night. We will keep the little one while you tend to your wife."

Lou gathered Willow in his arms. "Thank God, Willow. Thank God, you are all right."

One week later...

Missy and Willow walked out of Lori's Boutique with smiles on their faces. Lori had given Willow a light violet nightgown to replace the yellow one. 'To match her eyes', Lori had said. It was as sheer as the yellow that was ruined and had flowers the same as the other. Willow could not wait to surprise her husband with it, tonight. This was to be their night. It had been postponed, even though Willow had begged him not to. She was so excited, and her best friend was helping her. Ever the instigator, she had bought the bottle of wine. Kayla insisted it was straight from Paris. They would enjoy it at supper at Kayla's later.

Missy laughed gaily as she said, "Gabe will not care that I stick my oar in this time."

Willow agreed. Missy had baked Willow an apple pie for dessert later.

Missy gave her friend a hug. "I will be thinking about all the fun you two are having tonight." She turned with Starla and ran for home.

Willow laughed as she, too, ran home to hide the nightgown. This was to be a great surprise. She took a bath in her favorite rose water and dressed carefully. She sat in the rocker Lou had made for her last year. He'd made it extra big so he could hold her and rock her when she needed her papa. She leaned her head back, thinking how very lucky she was and how far they had come. She smiled as her eyes closed dreamily, lightly dozing, waiting for her papa to come home and take his little girl to dinner before his wife showed him how much she loved him and what a loving full-grown woman could do. She was both and she was immensely happy that way.

THE END

INTERESTING INFORMATION FROM THE AUTHOR

DOG FOOD

An American electrician, James Spratt, invented the first dog food. He was living in London while he watched dogs around a shipyard eating scraps of discarded biscuits. It wasn't long before he introduced his dog food, made up of wheat meals, vegetables and meat. This was in 1860 and was the beginning of the pet food industry.

In 1870, he went to New York and began the American pet food industry. He had the idea that he could make cheap, easy-to-use biscuits and then sell them to the urban dog owners. He had a simple recipe. It was a baked combination of wheat, beetroot and vegetables, bound together with beef blood.

ICE BOX

An icebox was a non-mechanical refrigerator. It was common in the early twentieth century as a way to keep food cool before there was electricity. It usually had a very pretty wood exterior, so if it was not used in the winter, it still looked nice in the kitchen and was used for storage.

Iceboxes had hollow walls that were lined with tin or zinc and packed with different insulation materials, such as sawdust or cork or straw or seaweed. The bottom held a large block of ice in a tray. Sometimes, the tray was in the top part. Cold air circulated around storage compartments on the inside. Some more expensive models had spigots for draining ice water from a catch pan or holding tank. In cheaper models, a drip pan was placed under the box and had to be emptied at least twice a day by hand. The user had to replace the melted ice, normally by obtaining new ice from an iceman who came in a wagon pulled by horses with large blocks of ice.

GAS STREETLIGHTS

In 1820, Paris started using gas lamps on the streets. Gas streetlights were put on posts and had to be lit every night and put out every morning. That was the job of 'lamp lighters', men or boys who went around and took care of the lights. They had to take care not to let too much gas into the lamp. If they did, when it was lit, it would explode. After that, gaslight spread to other countries.

Baltimore was the first city in the United States to have gas streetlights. Gas lamps were designed to be attractive for homes and on posts outside. Global usage of gas lamps on streets marks the beginning of the big gas companies.

Until the early twentieth century, most of the cities in America had gas streetlights and gas lamps in houses. Then electric light took over, and the gaslight was eliminated.

In the 1800s, Christmas became an important time for families to celebrate at home. More and more Americans began to follow the European traditions of Christmas trees and giving gifts. German immigrants brought their tradition of putting lights, sweets and toys on the branches of evergreen trees placed in their homes.

This tradition of setting up a Christmas tree soon spread to

INTERESTING INFORMATION FROM THE AUTHOR

many American homes. So did the practice of giving people presents. As these traditions increased in popularity, the modern trade and business linked to Christmas also grew.

As Christmas became more and more popular, some states declared the day a state holiday. Louisiana was the first state to make Christmas a holiday, in 1837. By 1860, fourteen other states had followed. It was not until 1870 that President Ulysses Grant made Christmas a federal holiday.

Americans already knew old Christmas songs that came from England and other areas of Europe. But many new American Christmas songs started to become popular. For example, in 1849, a minister from Massachusetts wrote the words to 'It Came Upon a Midnight Clear'. The song 'Jingle Bells' appeared seven years later. And, a year later, a religious leader in Williamsport, Pennsylvania wrote the song 'We Three Kings of Orient Are'.

And, of course, no Christmas would be complete without talking about one of the holiday's most famous traditions, Santa Claus.

CHAR CAULEY

I am a happily married mother of three sons and two kitties.
I live in a very small town (unincorporated) in Wisconsin.
I love to garden, write and of course read.
I also work in a glass factory with robots.
Writing is a lifelong dream come true.

Don't miss these exciting titles by Char Cauley and Blushing Books!

Healer Series
Amanda's Wolf – Book 1
Colleen's Laird – Book 2
Little Hope's Doctor – Book 3

Daughters of Samual Fox Series
Spring's Savior - Book 1
Summer's Lawman - Book 2
Autumn's Doctor - Book 3
Wynter's Storm - Book 4
Willow's Journey - Book 5

Audiobooks
Amanda's Wolf

Milton Keynes UK
Ingram Content Group UK Ltd.
UKHW030025180324
439604UK00001B/85